Karmveer Bhaurao Patil

Dr. D. T. Bhosale

**Translated from the Marathi by
Dr. Deepak Borgave**

Diamond Publications

Karmveer Bhaurao Patil

Dr. D. T. Bhosale

Translation : Dr. Deepak Borgave

First Edition : August , 2016

ISBN : 978-81-8483-682-0

© Diamond Publications

Cover Page
Sham Bhalekar

Typesetting
Sandhya Kamat

Published by
Diamond Publications
264/3 Shaniwar Peth, 302 Anugrah Apartment
Near Omkareshwar Temple, Pune - 411 030
☎ 020-24452387, 24466642
info@diamondbookspune.com
www.diamondbookspune.com

Sole Distributor :
Diamond Book Depot
661 Narayan Peth
Appa Balwant Chowk
Pune 411 030
Tel. - 24480677, 66020282

In Memory of Karmveer Bhaurao Patil

Holding the little Shahu finger
He walked his way;
He walked longer distances crust in the red mud.

As a young man, he saw a vision
Experimenting in his own capacity and power;
Lifting thousands of suns
At his shoulder
And sowing vibrant seeds
In millions of villages;

He produced millions of hands
Loyal armies made from unheard mud
With chalks as swords in their hands;
The hands that rocked the spirit of the orthodox
The hands that changed faces

Of bahujan and untouchables' cultures

He built schools in thousands of temples
And indulged in thousand temples of learning
Kids and boys cuddled at his shoulder;
He picked up a fistful of shining rays
From village mud
And wild plants from forests;

He planted them in his head
And
Willfully
Wandered like a storm
To shoot a revolution.

And he became a prophet
With the dream of Phule
Rolling
In his open veins of brain
And then he worked and worked and worked.

He trampled unknown ways;
He walked immeasurable distances
Incomprehensible to an ordinary soul;
His legs shattered to pieces
To shoot a revolution.

No funds, no money, no support drooping in his pocket;
The scorching sun
Hanging above his head;
But his wife was with him
Like a bright sun in his whirlwind;
So he didn't give up his silent prayers
And he pursued and pursued them
Till he found a wider realm
And
He groped strength and courage

From his little souls
Dangling in his windy head.

And then,
Every villager dropped a moon in his wallet
With smiling lights in their eyes.

Yes,
He did what he saw
As a working prophet and a nonchalant seer.
He served and served millions and millions
Till he grew an old man

And he spoke on education
Among illiterates and villagers,
In hills and mountains,
At farms and river sides
And at thousands of courtyards.
He trod the untrodden ways
Unknown to the educated
Ceaselessly.

He also spoke
Among the educated
And said,
That a true man lies within you
And
Outside the classrooms.

He was an activist
Speaking to the young and the old
Shredding vibrant energies
And illuminations in them.

Villagers and city men
Held him
Dispassionately in the beginning;

But later,
Each one
Dashed out at his altars
And mountains and hills splintered.

Sitting at a foot-hill
With his legs folded
He spoke again.
His soothing voice and flashed lights
Simmering corners of many eyes;
He gave each one a few seeds
And said,
"Take these...
And sow them at your shoulders
And
They will sprout out soon
Through your heads."
And each one
Sowed them at their shoulders
And the seeds
Sprouted out
Through their heads;

His eyes sparkled with hopes
And he was happy about them.
People called him Karmveer
A leader of the poor and depressed.

Germinations splashed and surfaced
And centuries of darkness dazzled out;
And then,
Huts and shanties began to scribble
And the speckled horizon
Simmered in laughter
At hill sides and huge mountains.

Yes!
He was a prophet
A working prophet and an activist
A Karmveer of his times
Speaking to the young and the old
Shredding vibrant energies
Speaking to classes and masses
Speaking to literates, illiterates, villagers and city men.

- Deepak Borgave

Foreword

Dr. D. T. Bhosale is a well known writer and critic in Marathi literature. His stories and novels are manifestations of rural life of Maharashtra. He has done some serious writings and it also presents issues of rural life. Besides, his writings show a sense of social commitment. Dr. Bhosale's *Lokottar*, (Sant Gadage Maharaj: Life and Works, 2007; Granthali) is an important book in Marathi literature. It has acquired recognition and acclaim in Maharashtra. Similarly, the biographical accounts of Karmveer Bhaurao Patil recorded in the book, *Kumaranche Karmveer* has also acquired recognition and acclaim. This book is specifically written for the adolescent readers; the title in Marathi implies it. The adolescent reader is a sensitive growing person; he or she is about to enter the most windy age. Their world is different from children's world. It is indeed a challenging task for a writer to enter their world. So a writer has to take care of several things while he speaks to an adolescent reader. Whether it is meant for children or adolescents, inculcation of values becomes an important aspect in writing such books because these readers are going to be tomorrow's responsible citizens. Such readers assume responsible roles in future.

Maharashtra is known as a progressive state in our country. This is indeed true if we neglect a few exceptional things. The Maharashtra that we see today has not been produced so easily. This is obviously true of any state or region. We have to turn to the nineteenth century Maharashtra to understand its progressive aspects. In this context, Mahatma Jyotirao Phule is the most important revolutionary thinker-activist. He spent his entire life to end the centuries old enslavement of the people. The education of women and the Bahujan communities was the most important agenda of social revolution. Without education we cannot liberate men and women. Phule had understood it very clearly. So he started schools for women and untouchables. This was the beginning of the social revolution in Maharashtra. Rajarshi Shahu Maharaj and Vitthal Ramaji Shinde took this revolution to a further stage. They put in their significant contributions in it. But it was Karmveer Bhaurao Patil who put in concrete and substantial contributions in this direction. He took a big leap in the realm of education and perfected the revolution that Phule had initiated during the nineteenth century Maharashtra. Mahatma Phule and Karmveer Bhaurao Patil's contributions have formed today's Maharashtra. Dr. Babasaheb Ambedkar added some dynamism to the transformations that both Phule and Karmveer had ensued. We are today freed from the semi-feudal mentality; it is because of these social changes. Nevertheless, the signs and symbols of the feudal mentality are even alive in us to some extent. But in course of time, let us hope that we shall do away with them.

Karmveer Bhaurao Patil had his own social and educational perceptions. He had also his own philosophy of education. When he started his work in the field of education, the society was engulfed by illiteracy, backwardness and ignorance. He literally walked down thousands of miles in rural regions to understand the social and political phenomena. He brought with him hundreds of children to Satara for their education. He took their responsibility. If you want to give education to such rural children, you need to have boarding, where the children can stay and seek education. So before he opened schools, he opened boarding. He moved door to door and begged for donations. Historical heroes are persons who change the course of human history. Karmveer was one such modern historical hero who changed social and cultural history of Maharashtra.

He started a novel scheme called *Earn while Learn*. By doing so, he integrated labour and knowledge together. He said that if you want to make education meaningful, you must bring labour and education together. A student cannot become a bookish worm then. The scheme helped learners to complete their education. But most important thing was that the students achieved self pride. This was a revolutionary development in the educational history of modern India. In one way, we can understand it as a development of bloodless revolution achieved through peace.

A revolutionary seldom gets an opportunity to taste the fruits the revolution. A revolutionary had to walk a thorny road. Karmveer walked all his life such thorny roads. He was neither a king, a landlord nor any Maharaja. He lived all his life fighting against odds. He collected fistful of grains from each door where he started schools and made arrangements of a day's meals for his children. He followed some principles while he did these things. Whatever he got through dominations, he never used it in his personal life. It was meant for children and he used it for them. He sold his wife's golden ornaments, his personal possessions from his home to continue education of his boarding boys. This is eccentric enough if we look at today's educational barons. Today's educational barons do not worry about whether their students get their daily bread or not in their hostels, or whether their teachers get regular salaries or not; but there must be weighty golden ornaments tucked at their wives' neck. That is more important for them. Such barons are abundant enough around us these days.

Karmveer himself was a man of principles. He believed in self respect and so he wanted his students to respect themselves and principles. As a Minister of Maharashtra, Morarjibhai Desai stopped the grants of Karmveer's Rayat Shikshan Sanstha. This was the result of some misunderstanding between the government and Karmveer. But Bhaurao Patil was not scared. He did not surrender before anyone even in unfavourable times. He described his students as dollars. This is possible only for a principled man like Karmveer Bhaurao Patil. Hundreds of people took inspiration from him and worked in the field of education after him.

It is necessary that we must introduce such uncommon peoples' lives and their works and contributions to the young readers of today. Life stories of such heroes can inculcate values among the young generation of today. It is often said that there are no ideals today where you find complete solace. This is true in some sense. But it is also true that we have great historical heroes as high as Himalaya like Mahatma Phule, Mahatma Gandhi, Dr. Ambedkar, Vitthal Ramaji Shinde and Karmveer Bhaurao Patil. These personalities have always been respectable and admirable persons to us. This list can be a little lengthened. But that is not necessary here. These are our ideals and we must think that they must be ideals before the upcoming generations. Primarily, Dr. D. T. Bhosale has written the book, *Kumaranche Karmveer* with this social and moral purpose in his mind. He did not write the book only because he was serving in Rayat Shikshan Sanstha. He wrote it simply because it has a sense of social commitment. And therefore the book has acquired some value and meaning in course of time.

One more aspect of Dr. Bhosale's personality as an author is that he is a literary writer. He was therefore able to understand the world of the young people. He could write such a book because he knew well the emotional world of adolescent readers. When such books are written, a writer has to be very conscious about the language he exploits in a book. Dr. Bhosale has developed a simple style in this book, so that his readers can digest it comfortably. Dr. Bhosale has been successful in his attempts.

Dr. Deepak Borgave, my friend, has translated this book in English. This is a significant act from different points of view. Dr. Borgave is a bilingual poet; he writes in Marathi and English. Besides, whatever works he has translated till now, he has done it with a sense of social commitment. He has been engaged in translation activities since a long time with the same perception. He is besides a certified translator; he has received rigorous training in translation studies. He holds a Ph. D. in Translation Studies. He translates Marathi texts in English and vice versa. In this series, he has translated *Kumaranche Karmveer* in English. Translating a text in an alien language like English is a very difficult job. This is not possible for a naïve person. It requires wider experience as a translator. And Dr. Borgave has acquired it. Moreover, you need to have command over the target language. He has acquired it by his own efforts as he has wider experience in the art of translation.

Translation of such a book in English has one more important aspect. We see that today the English medium schools are increasing in good numbers even in towns and semi-rural areas. Some of them are very expensive schools. There are several questions that one can ask in this context. Do these schools have any standards? Do we argue favourably that English can be indeed a medium of knowledge acquisition? Or don't we think that knowledge acquisition can be easier in mother tongue instruction? There are several such problems that we can visualize in this context. Obviously, this is not a place where we should answer such questions. Perhaps, the time itself will answer these questions. But we cannot neglect the fact that the English medium schools are increasing in a wider scale. Students from middle classes and even lower middle classes are seeking education in such schools. This is again a reality we cannot neglect. Is it not our responsibility then to introduce them important personalities of Maharashtra? Is it not our job to inculcate in them values that these social revolutionaries, reformers and thinkers had produced in their life times? We have to produce good readers for tomorrow's world. This is our moral responsibility. If we don't do it, then they will just keep saying 'yes' and 'no' only. Good books in English are necessary for producing ideal citizens. Social and cultural organizations must come forward to fulfill this need. The government also must take initiatives in this direction and work out such plans and schemes and produce good literature in English.

If such things are going to happen tomorrow, one can say that Dr. Deepak Borgave has done some pioneering work in this sphere. If history records it, then Dr. Borgave's efforts will not be wasted.

Dr. Nagnath Kottapalle
Former Vice Chancellor,
Bharatratna Dr. Babasaheb Ambedkar
Marathwada University,
Aurangabad

Preface

I feel extremely happy to hand over the English translation of my biographical text *Kumaranche Karmveer* to the readers. Dr. Deepak Borgave had translated the book long back in 2004 but for one or the other reason, its publication was postponed. I am very happy that it is being published now. I congratulate Dr. Borgave who took strenuous efforts to transfer the source text and brought its main thrust in the English language.

The Marathi book was first published by Rayat Shikshan Sanstha's academic wing, Karmveer Vidya Prabodhini in 1988; later it was reprinted in 2011. The people involved in the Prabodhini thought that a biography of Karmveer could be important in the episodic form for the adolescent readers. The Prabodhini wanted the student community to understand Karmveer's life and works and identify his place in today's social and political scenario. I too had the same motive behind writing of this book. That was how the Marathi book came into being. The book received a wider acclaim and recognition outside the Rayat family over a period of time..

The main purpose of the venture was to introduce the readers, Karmveer's stormy life, his philosophy of education, the significance of his contributions in the field of education; its impact on the political, social and economic life of Maharashtra and our country. Most important perception was to familiarize the readers the values, attitudes, dignity of labour, sell-help, earn and learn and the very ways of living that Karmveer wanted to inculcate among the bahujan and dalit communities. The significant events chosen from Karmveer's life compose the main substance of the book.

The English translation of this book is very important event for me. Today's educational scene has drastically undergone a rapid change. The speed with which the scene is changing is beyond one's imagination. In such a rapid changing era, the importance of the English language is increasing though we may not wish. It has become the need of the time. The transition activity has therefore has become unprecedentedly significant. In such a cultural scenario, Marathi texts are not being translated in English in the proportion that we need to do it. My book in such a situation has been translated in English. This is indeed a thing of joy for me.

I acknowledge assistance from Barrister P. G. Patil, Dr. N. D. Patil, Adv. Raosaheb Shinde, M. B. Katkar, Principal Ghate, Principal R. D. Gaikwad, V. V. Pandit and the writers of the reference books on Karmveer Bhaurao Patil. I thank them all.

July 2016   **Dr. D.T. Bhosale,**
                                  Pandharpur

Translator's Note

During the last two and half decades, there has been a significant rise in the English readership. The globalization processes, the developments nurtured by science and technology, computerization of every aspect of life and scores of other things have accelerated use of English in our country. Today, we find the children playing with mobile phones. This is because of the rapid changes in the spheres of mobile technology. We therefore find today easy availability of android mobile phones, easy access to social networking like WhatsApp and Facebook; it has consequently increased greater amount of exposure to the English language among the young people of today. In the last decade, the Government of Maharashtra introduced English as a compulsory subject from the first standard in the primary schools of the state. This decision was taken perhaps in the context of the recent global developments and increasing use of English across the country.

Translations of Marathi texts are also significantly on the rise during the last two and half decades. The present attempt is a manifestation of the complex linguistic processes. I have a feeling that the present target text can be useful for school and college going students of Marathi as well as English medium schools. At the same time, it can be an introduction to Karmveer Bhaurao Patil's life and works.

I was a colleague of Dr. D. T. Bhosale in Annasaheb Awate College and Pandharpur College in 1980's. These colleges are well known branches of Rayat Shikshan Sanstha. I worked with Dr. Bhosale as co-editor of the college annuals. He appeared to me an amicable person. I did not know then that he was a well known Marathi writer, critic and an influential personality in the literary circles of Maharashtra.

The source text, *Kumaranche Karmveer* is meant for the adolescent readers. I remember it well that I gave it to my school going son before two decades while he was preparing to participate in an elocution contest on Karmveer. Dr. Bhosale wrote it in the episodic form, so that it would appeal to the adolescent consciousness. I never had even a bleak idea that I might translate the same in English.

There are several books in English on Karmveer Bhaurao Patil. Unfortunately such rich and scholarly writings do not reach the young readers. And even if they get it, they do not dare to read it looking at its voluminous size and complexity. I therefore decided to translate this book for the adolescent readers.

Objectives such as to provide graded reading material in English, to introduce life and works of Karmveer Bhaurao Patil and his ideas and philosophy of education were in my mind while translating it.

I took maximum efforts to achieve equivalence in the target text while transferring the source text. I feel confident that the readers might welcome my venture.

At the very outset, I must thank Honourable Dr. Anil Patil, Chairman, Rayat Shikshan Sanstha, Satara who unhesitatingly gave me permission for the English translation of this book. I must also thank Respected Shri. Vijay Kolate, the Managing Council Member, Rayat Shikshan Sanstha, Satara who met Dr. Patil in this context and took initiatives in this direction.

Dr. D. T. Bhosale, the source text writer, had been an inspirational force to me in this venture. I thank him for the same.

I thank several dignitaries of the Sanstha who encouraged me to take such a project. I thank Dr. N. D. Patil, former Chairman, Rayat Shikshan Sanstha, Satara, Adv. Raosaheb Shinde, former Chairman, Rayat Shikshan Sanstha, Adv. Ram Kandge, Chairman, Western Region, Advisory Committee, Pune and Managing Council Member, Rayat Shikshan Sanstha, Principal R. K. Shinde, Director of Karmveer Vidya Prabodhini, Dr. Ganesh Thakur, Secretary, Rayat Shikshan Sanstha, Dr. D. D. Patil, Joint Secretary, Principal Uttam Awari, Joint Secretary, Chandrakant Jadhav, Inspector, Western Division, Pune. Rayat Shikshan Sanstha and Dr Ashok Bhoite, former Pro-Vice Chancellor of Shivaji University, Kolhapur, and Principal of Mahatma Phule Mahavidyalaya, Pimpri, Pune.

I thank Shri Ramesh Deshmane of Kolhapur for his valuable assistance in re-drawing the pictures for the English edition.

I also would like to thank Dr. Nagnath Kottapalle, former Vice-Chancellor of Bharatratna Dr. Babasaheb Ambedkar Marathwada University, Aurangabad, Principal, Dr. Arun Andhale, Principal, Dr. Rajeev Bawadhankar, Principal Dr. Shirish Chindhade, Dr. Dilip Chavan, School of Language and Culture Studies, Swami Ramanand Teerth Marathwada University, Nanded, Dr. Manohar Jadhav, Dean of the Faculty of Fine Arts, Savitribai Phule Pune University, Subhash Thorat and Kiran Moghe, social activists, Mangesh Narayanrao Kale, Prof. Suhas Nirmale, Dr. Rajan Gavas, Head, Department of Marathi, Shivaji University, Kolhapur, Dr. Chandrakant Langare, Department of English, Shivaji University, Kolhapur, Dr. Sunil Sawant, Department of English, Kisan Veer Mahavidyalaya, Wai,

Dr. Anil Pharakate, Department of English, Kankawali College, my colleagues from Mahatma Phule Mahavidyalaya, Dr. Pramod Botre, Dr. Jayashri Magdum, Prof. Sunil Ghanwat, Prof. Ayyub Shaikh, Prof. Tulshidas Aphale, Prof. Shahaji Karande, Dr. Ramesh Randive, Dr. Babasaheb Shendge, Prof. Dinkar Murkute, Prof. Rajendra Bawale and Dr. Pandurang Bhosale. Finally, I thank Shri Dattatray Pasthe of Diamond Publications, Pune and his staff for publication of this book.

I dedicate this book to my elder son, Dr. Vivek Borgave.

Jai Karmveer!

July 2016

Dr. Deepak Borgave,
Department of English,
Mahatma Phule Mahavidyalaya, Pune .
Res. : Bhaktinandan, S. N. 1/2/31,
Near Mahadev Mandir, Mamata Nagar,
Old Sangvi, Pune- 411027;
Mob: 09422518864

Our country is composed of plenty of villages. Maharashtra must have more than seven lacks of villages and *Wadi-vastis*. Aaitawade is one of such villages located in the southern part of the former Satara district. Today, it is in Walwa tehsil of Sangali district. Away from the highway and city-hubs, Aaitawade is well known for its odds and inconveniences. This village is known for its fertility of land. If you sow a man here, he might come out of it and grow as big as a tree. Therefore, the village was identified as banana Aaitawade. Banana and *Pan* (eating leaves) have been the staple agricultural produce of the village. A farmer of the village was happy and satisfied man on his agricultural produce. He did not meddle in any other affairs. He worked hard at his farm all day and produced whatever was possible for him. This was the norm of the village. Caste differences were observed and followed in the village.

A man called Devgauda Patil lived in this village. He was a distinguished well known person. His forefathers came from Karnataka that is Bijapur district. The village was known by the name Mudbidri. Probably, the forefathers of the Patil family must have migrated to this village in search of work and employment. With consistent efforts, the family achieved name and *Patilaki* and some land and property. The family belonged to the Jain creed. The Jains are hard working people and they are free from addictions. The character of family was remarkable. They were religious minded people. They greeted guests wholeheartedly and made them as comfortable as possible. Devgauda Patil was a man of culture.

The family was rich. It had a higher status in the society. Devgauda was a distinguished man in the *Matha* (a Jain Monastery) of the Jain community in Kolhapur. He fastened a large hanky around his head. So people fondly called him, *Rumalgaunda* (Rumal is a sort of handkerchief). He participated in various activities of the Matha in Kolhapur with *Swami* (religions priest).

Once a quarrel was brought to the Matha and Swami and other members found a way out. As a result, the conflict was brought to a friendly solution. Devegauda was the member of the the Math. The Swami requested him to sign the document. The Swami said, "Now Gauda, sign this document."

"My God! What a problem? Who knows how to sign? This is an awkward position among the people!" Devegaunda felt ashamed and humiliated. He suddenly got up, leaving the meeting of the Matha and reached his village, Aaitawade. He called up his son who had just started going to school. He said, "See Paygauda, you give up all farm work, you have to learn more and more and become a great man."

He sent his son to a town, so that he can continue his education. Thus, the father instead of giving wealth to his son, he gave him the third eye, the eye of knowledge.

RAMESH
DESHMANE

Paygauda passed the sixth standard examination. It was the final vernacular examination in those days. As soon as he passed the exam, he got a job in the revenue department. Paygauda was a patient, upright and disciplined man. He had twelve rupees as the monthly salary. He did not spend all the money but saved some amount monthly from it. Gangubai, his wife was a good person in household works. She came from Kumbhoj. She was the favorite daughter of her father,

Jingauda Patil. Her family was rich but it was very orthodox. Bhaurao was born on 22 September 1887 to this couple. He was the eldest son. He was his mother's favorite son and he also loved his mother very much. During her old age and sickness, Bhaurao served and nursed her.

Paygauda was transferred to different places such as Islampur, Vita, Dahiwadi, Karad as a government servant. He took all possible care, so that his son's education should not disturb. Bhaurao was a mischievous and rebellious by nature. He took initiatives and led in several things other than school and his studies. He played among all sorts of boys and brought unexpected quarrels to home. Practice of untouchability was common in those days. People observed it intensely. Even shadows of untouchables were considered unholy and polluting holiness of *Savarn* communities. But Bhaurao was not afraid of any consequences and he played with the untouchable boys fearlessly. He took their sides and felt hurt if untouchables were treated badly.

Once, when Bhau was at Vita, he wandered all day with one of his Mahar friends. When they felt thirsty, they came at a public well. The people were fetching water at the well. When they saw Bhau with a Mahar boy, they said they would give water to Bhau but not the Mahar boy. They refused to give water from the well to the Mahar boy. Bhau was adamant. He asked what was going to happen if his Mahar friend came near to the well and the bucket or the rope used for fetching the water. How these will be polluted? He told them that they both would drink the water at one time. The people at the well were shocked and they shouted. They opposed him severely. As a result, thirsty Bhau too did not get the water.

Bhau was not only adamant but he was emphatic in certain matters. He asked them resolutely why the untouchables were not allowed to drink water of the public well. His face was reddened because of intense anger. The intense annoyance was reflected in his eyes. He thought for a moment and within a second, he let the rope roll down in the well. There was no chance left for the people at the well to fetch water from the well. He asked the people to fetch water as much as they wanted and drink it as much as they felt. Saying so, he ran homeward as fast as he could. He narrated the entire episode to mother. While narrating, he breathed hard.

A similar kind of event took place when he was at Karad. Bhaurao's mother had been to fetch water at a well. It was a well reserved for the Brahmin community. Bhau's mother Gangubai was a religious woman by nature. She was orthodox and she would not tolerate, if someone touched her pitcher. A Brahmin boy, to tease Gangubai touched the pitcher. Gangubai patiently poured the water and washed her pitcher once again and refilled it. But the boy was mischievous and he repeated it seven to eight times, just to harass her. When Bhau came to know about it, what he did was that he invited his friends from different castes and creeds and told them to fetch water from the well which was reserved for the Brahmin community.

He ordered the boys, "Fetch water from this well. This is our well. Water does not hold any caste." Bhau attempted two things through this act of rebellion. He took revenge upon the Brahmin boy who teased his mother and opened the well to all castes. It was act of social change in those days. It was as well an act of social revolution.

Bhaurao did such odd things right from his childhood. If he did not agree with something and if he found something unjust, he went against it.

Bhaurao was studying in a Marathi school. When he got less mark in a particular subject, his teacher promoted him to the next class. This was how his school education was in progress. He completed his education up to the fifth standard at Vita. Since there was no facility of further education at Vita, the neighbours and a few friends suggested to his father that he must send Bhaurao to Kolhapur. This was how Bhaurao came to Jain Boarding in Kolhapur.

Rajarshi Shahu Maharaj was the chief of the Kolhapur Sansthan. His contribution in the field of education, sport and art was immense. He took efforts to eradicate untouchability. He tried to minimize the impact of orthodox religion and ignorance that was rooted in the minds of the people of his Sansthan. He built separate boarding for each cast and community. They were free of charges. These boardings were for the rural students of the region who came to Kolhapur for their further education. Bhaurao's education continued without much hassle because of the boarding facilities available in the Shahu Maharaja's Sansthan.

Once, Bhaurao was going from Kolhapur to meet his parents. Then, his parents were staying at Islampur. It was a vacation time, so there were no classes. As he was passing from a primary school, he saw a very interesting picture. The teacher was teaching in the class. The boys in the classroom were listening to the teacher with concentration. But one boy was sitting outside the classroom; he was almost in the veranda. He too was listening to the teacher attentively. There was plenty of street noise but it did not disturb the boy because he was very much concentrative.

As Bhaurao saw it, he rushed into the classroom and shouted against the teacher, "Why do you keep this boy outside the classroom?"

The teacher was confused to see a well built youth, talking to him in high pitch sound. The teacher did not know what to say. However, he managed to explain to him, "The boy is from the Mahar community and how can I allow him to sit inside the classroom with other boys?" Bhaurao talked to the teacher for a long time and convinced him. It was not his fault that he was born in the Mahar community. He erased the opinions of the teacher. He gave him rational and logical explanations. But what a poor teacher can do? He was under pressures of the orthodox religion. He was helpless. He agreed with Bhaurao. He said, "What you are saying is entirely right, my boy; but how can I allow him to sit inside the classroom? I'm helpless because of the social situation."

"Come, my friend. Don't get embarrassed. I shall make better arrangements for your school", said Bhaurao and he took him to his home. He asked to sit with him for meals in his home and while going out, he informed mother that the boy belonged to the Mahar caste. He took him to Kolhapur. There was a boarding in Kolhapur; its name was Miss Clarke Boarding. It was meant for *Harijan* boys. The boy got admission in the boarding. The name of this boy was Dnyandev Gholap. Later, he became an editor and an MLA. He became an activist and a true follower of Bhaurao in future. It was the first experiment of Bhaurao in education. It provided him a source of inspiration in future to work in the field of education.

Rebellious temperament was perhaps Bhaurao's second nature. He went against something in which he did not believe or something which was not good for human beings. He did not care of what might happen or what might be its consequences. He fought against religion, traditions, customs and man's selfish nature. He did not pay attention to meaningless customs.

It is a general rule that we usually follow. For instance, when we are in a boarding for the purpose of education, obviously we follow the norms and conventions of the boarding. At times, we adjust to a new situation. Bhaurao also should have followed the rules when he was in the Jain boarding. This is what we might think; but it is a selfish thought to serve our selfish ends. So, it did not happen with Bhaurao. It was not his nature to adapt to unjust practices. He never made compromises for trivial reasons like 'shaving in time' or 'bathing for second time' etc. And for not following such rules of the boarding, he had to pay a huge price. He had to leave the boarding. Subsequently, he had to give up his education once and for all.

Bhaurao was at Jain boarding in Kolhapur. There was a general rule of the boarding that the students must shave before they took meals. Any boy was not allowed to shave after the meals. The head of the boarding was Annasaheb Latthe. He was one of the prominent administrative officers of the Kolhapur Sansthan. He was as well a distinguished and respected personality in the Jain community. Later on, he became the Minister of Education in the Bombay State.

Bhaurao knew the rule; he had read it several times displayed in the notice-board. Yet he shaved after the meals. He kept this practice for a few days deliberately. Mr. Latthe came to know about it. He took Bhaurao to task. Without getting scared of what Latthe said, Bhaurao informed him coolheadedly, "There is no any rule about shaving in Jain religion, I feel."

"You don't have to tell me all that, I know it."

"Then what is going to happen if one shaves after meals?"

"This is the rule of the Boarding. You see, a rule is a rule. No one is allowed to break it." Latthe said sternly.

"Is that so? Then do you follow these rules?" Bhaurao turned the entire game against the officer.

He continued, "If the head of the boarding is not following the rule, how do you force boys to follow it? I'll not follow the rule."

Such a response of Bhaurao obviously shocked everyone including the officer. After a few days, a similar kind of event took place. Shahu Maharaj of Kolhapur had started a separate boarding for the untouchables. The boarding was named after the Governor's daughter, Miss Clarke. She was a social worker and an activist in the social field. Shahu Maharaj himself attended the function. Bhaurao too attended it. The boarding officer did not like this act of Bhaurao. He ordered his cook to stop serving him his regular meals. Later on, after consulting others, he allowed Bhaurao to take his meals, if he bathes before the meals. But Bhaurao was a rebel. He did not obey the orders. He flatly said, "I will not bathe again."

"You have to take bath; you attended a programme of the untouchable community."

"I do not believe in untouchability and will never do so in future. They are also human beings and not animals." Bhaurao was firm in him opinion.

"Yes, you are right. But they belong to untouchable castes."

"But I don't feel it appropriate to bathe when I come in contact with them." Bhaurao was very rational.

"Then you will not get your meals." said a neighboring boy.

"But I will eat my meals." Bhaurao spoke in the same tone.

"You will not get the meals at all. The kitchen is locked", the boy looked victorious.

"Is that so? I'll see, how I could you stop me from getting my meals?' Saying so, Bhaurao broke one of the windows of the kitchen and straight-a-way entered the kitchen. He was very much hungry. He sat comfortably in the kitchen and devoured on whatever came to his lot. He ate till his belly was full and then went out of the kitchen.

What were its consequences? Bhaurao was expelled from the Boarding. The administrative officer, Latthe told him to leave the boarding at once. His entire belongings were thrown out of the Boarding and he got the reward of his behaviour against the authority.

Shahu Maharaj came to know about it and when he asked about it, Latthe said, "This boy is not disciplined; he is very loose in behaviour. His temperament is rude. If such a boy might be in the boarding, other boys will imitate him. So, it is not good to keep him in the boarding." Thus, the boarding life of Bhaurao came to an end at this juncture of time.

Bhjaurao's hostel life came to an end but Shahu Maharaj brought him to his palace. He was accompanied by his classmate. His name was Balasaheb Khanvilkar. He started staying in his room. Balasaheb was a close relative to the Maharaj. Both of them stayed together and enjoyed facilities of the palace. Maharaja was non-vegetarian. On some occasions, he went out for lunch or dinner. He was very much fond of physical exercise. *Pahilwans* from different regions came to him for his patronage. He organized wrestling contests in Kolhapur.

It was compulsory for the boys staying in the palace to take physical exercises regurarly. Khanvilkar did not have much interest in such exercises. But Bhaurao liked physical exercises very much. Maharaja made arrangements for special food to such boys. The food consisted of such items as milk, *pista*, ghee, almond etc. Such food was known as *khurak*. Bhaurao enjoyed it and also devoured on Khanvilkar's lot! The result was that his physic developed rapidly and he became a strong well-built youth. His arms grew well shaped like a good wrestler. On some occasions, he massaged the Maharaja. He drank about one and half litre of milk and ate special *khurak* everyday preserved for him.

On one day, the Maharaja asked him, "You appear

to be a well built boy. Why don't you join our *talim* (gym) now?"

"Yes Maharaj, I will."

"I will make you the best wrestler. I will appoint the best teacher (*Vastad*) for you. You must take part in wrestling contests and win medals for me."

"Yes Maharaj!" answered Bhaurao.

Sometimes, Bhaurao played cricket with boys of the palace. Once, while he was batting, he hit the ball brilliantly. It fell on the window panes of the palace and the glasses broke into pieces. The boys got scared thinking that the Maharaja will be very angry upon them.

The Maharaja called the boys and asked them about who were playing the cricket. Bhaurao replied, "We, the boys of the palace, Maharaja."

"Who hit the ball? Is this the way you play cricket?"

"Maharaj, the glasses were broken by the ball I hit it. I didn't know that the ball might go so high." Bhaurao narrated the truth.

"Humn... so you did the crime!" Maharaj was still in his angry mood.

"Yes Maharaj! But I didn't do it deliberately. Whatever punishment you give, I shall accept it."

When Bhaurao said so, the face of Maharaja tamed down. He began to smile as he saw the boy was boldly narrating the truth. He said, "You are not afraid of me?"

"Maharaj, what fear is there? Whatever has happened, one must narrate it truthfully, and be ready for punishment. What fear is there in it?"

"That's good. I excuse you because you speak from the depth of your heart. Now, run all of you to your places."

Bhaurao narrated the entire story to his friends. To speak truth was his natural temperament. So he never learnt the art of telling lies.

Once, the Maharaja found that a few boys were smoking cigarettes. He called all of them and asked each about who were smoking cigarettes.

"Who was smoking? Say a...a..."

"Not me...not me... Maharaj. Except me all were smoking."

"Yes Maharaj."

"Except me, all were smoking."

Everybody gave the same answer. Bhaurao also gave the same answer. Bhaurao did not smoke at all. Maharaj knew well that even if this boy faced a death punishment, he would never tell lies.

Bhaurao's stay in the palace was of greater advantage. He saw the Maharaja closely. He came to know his views and opinions on social reformation. Mahatma Phule and his views were introduced to Bhaurao through the Maharaj. He saw efforts of the Maharaja in the field of education and social reformation for the untouchables. One must devote one's life for the welfare of others; this was the ideal of the Maharaja's life. It imprinted deeply in Bhaurao's mind. He learnt such several things in his stay at the palace. He developed his physical status as a well-built young man in the palace days.

Bhaurao did not have much interest in studies, but he excessively loved physical exercises. Moreover, the best food was available to him in the palace. Besides, there was no fear of failure in the school studies. Then, how would Bhaurao take extra pains for the study! He studied whatever was possible in the regular classes during the school time. English and Mathematics were very difficult subjects for him. They were his number one enemies. He was somehow successful in these subjects up to the fifth standard, but he got stuck in the sixth standard. He failed in the subjects. The Maharaja came to know about it. He thought that Bhaurao was a good wrestler; he was besides a boy of many virtues. So he had a soft corner for him. Thinking that he could do something for him, he called his teacher. His teacher's name was Bhargavram Kulkarni. He told the teacher to promote him to the next class. Bhaurao too secretly thought that the teacher might not hesitate to follow Maharaja's request.

The Maharaja said to the teacher, "This is Bhau Patil! Your student."

"Yes Maharaja. I know him."

"Then, can you help him? He has some difficulty. Can you promote him to ...?"

The Maharaja stopped for a while. The teacher said, "Maharaj, this student is very weak in his studies. He must continue to study in the sixth class itself." While the teacher spoke, he put plenty of force on each of the syllable. He continued, "I shall rather move the desk, this boy used to sit in, to the next class instead of promoting him to the seventh class. I can promote the desk but not the boy. If the boy is promoted now, he will have to appear for matriculation examination for several times."

The Maharaj did not say anything for some time and then he turned to Bhaurao, "Bhau, what your teacher says is correct. You continue to study in the sixth standard this year."

Bhaurao nodded his head. Having little interest in the school studies and as he found learning in school was a matter of annoyance, he bid farewell to the school permanently.

Bhaurao, who had failed in English in the sixth standard, was awarded D. Litt. Degree by University of Pune in 1959. He established Rayat Shikshan Sanstha and provided the best education to hundreds and thousands of students. He also sent some of the students abroad for advanced studies. Had Bhaurao passed in the sixth class, what would have happened? He would have probably completed his matriculation education and he might have become a *Raosaheb* (a government clerk). He would not have become a 'Bhausaheb' and *Karmveer*. His failure became the principal cause of his future success.

Dr. Radhakrishnan, the President of India, visited Kolhapur. A programme was organized. Many distinguished personalities attended it. Bhaurao was also present on the occasion as an educationist. He had just recovered from some sickness. Everyone was introducing oneself as 'I'm a Justice', 'I'm a Doctor, 'I'm an Engineer', 'I'm an Industrialist' etc, When Bhaurao's turn came, he stood up, taking support of the stick and said, "Dr. Radhakrishnan, in the group of today's distinguished personalities, I'm a very different kind of bird whose feathers do not match to those of the present here. I do not feel any kind of hesitation in saying that while I was the student of Rajaram High School; I never passed in all subjects every year. Even then, I am a polite follower of Shahu Maharaj and Mahatma Gandhi. I established Rayat Shikshan Sanstha to pursue their ideals. Today, hundreds and thousands of students are seeking education in this Sanstha. Today, there are many schools of the Sanstha working in the thirteen districts of Maharashtra."

Dr. Radhakrishnan was moved by the words of Bhaurao. He was overwhelmed by his honest admission and sincere submission. He said "It's good Bhaurao that you failed in English. Had you passed the matriculation exam, you would have led your life as a common clerk. But today, you are making lives of hundreds and thousands of the poor students. This is indeed a huge task you are performing. You have changed the course of history. I've a feeling that I'm proud of your work. Let me pray to God to give you maximum strength so that you can carry the missionary work to your maximum capacity."

The hall reverberated with uninterrupted applause. Bhaurao left the school and he was a dropout. But he went on establishing more and more schools for the poor and the needy. That was how he later earned the title of *Karmveer*.

Bhaurao was eighteen years old when he left the school. Eighteen years was then a marriageable age. In those days, many boys got married even before they reached age of eighteen. Bhaurao got married when he was eighteen years old. His mother chose Akkada of the Patil family from Kumbhoj as her daughter-in-law. Akkada was the most appropriate match for Bhaurao as per the customs of the days. She was skilled in household work and cooking. The marriage ceremony took place at Kumbhoj.

Bhaurao had left the school. He had no job and in such a situation he was pushed into a status of a married man. Akkada after marriage become Laxmibai. Her name was not only changed but her entire life went under transformation beyond her imagination. She was later on identified as *Vahini* and then played a role of *Mauli* (Mother) and was a great supporting force to innumerable boys of the boarding. She was like mother to all of them.

Bhaurao left the school and a question stood before him about what he could do. Moreover, he was married and he had stepped into a marital status. So, he had new responsibilities on his shoulder. He thought of going for some job. He was confused however about what he could do. A conference of Jain community was organized at Kolhapur at this turn of time,. He worked as a volunteer in this conference. A diamond dealer, Seth Manikchand Hirachand met Bhaurao. He was happy to find Bhaurao as a trustworthy boy for his profession. He asked him if he could join him and work in his business at Mumbai. Bhaurao did not know what to say.

"I shall take care of your further education. You work with me in my business." Bhaurao had no work, so he said, "Yes, I'm ready. I will come with you."

And Bhaurao left for Mumbai. The Seth admitted him in a small commerce school to provide him with a short course in business. He was given a scholarship of thirty rupees. But Bhaurao could not complete the course. He left that school also. The Seth later on asked Bhaurao to work as a salesman in his shop. In the presence of diamonds and jewels, he was not happy. He could find no interest in the job. The Seth said, "Bhau, try to do the job carefully, you will earn lacks of rupees in this business."

"Sethji, I really don't find myself comfortable in the company of diamonds and jewels."

"My boy, in the beginning everyone feels so......if you want I'll give you some part of profit in your name."

"Shetaji, you really love me, your affection and favour makes me feel grateful and obliged to you, But....."

"Bhau, listen to me, so much less work and more money, you'll not get in any business."

The Seth tried to convince him in every possible way and Bhaurao was under his pressure of favour, so he too was not prepared to say no to the Shetaji.

"Shetaji, this Mumbai climate doesn't suit me and this job, this work is something I don't like." Somehow Bhaurao was able to voice his opinion.

"Then you take your decision", the Seth finally

advised him, though he was sad enough about his decision.

Bhaurao took the decision to go back to home. When he came back to the home, his father was in Koregaon. Bhaurao had no school, no job and there were plenty of family responsibilities waiting for him. Again hunting for job began.

"Bhau, you now work as a clerk in my office." Father said angrily.

"I 'm ready, that will do", replied Bhaurao and he started as a clerk in his father's office. However, the work bored him very soon. Sitting in a darkened room all day long just moving yellow sheets of paper up and down, he was upset. He left that job too. His father became sad on his son's decision. Then Bhaurao decided to get into the police force but his father opposed. Then he thought of joining the military to which his father again opposed. Then Bhaurao made attempts to establish an agricultural society. It was the First World War period and several of the society members had joined the army. That was how the society did not sustain and it collapsed before its birth.

Thus wherever Bhaurao tried his hand, he was unsuccessful. His entire life was darkened under a roof of several failures. He could not understand what he could do. At the same time, he found it very difficult to just lie down in the home without work and job. He became restless. It disturbed him entirely. The only question that troubled him was what he could do in his near future.

Some events appear very trivial but they become turning points in our life. Such events appear ordinary but they bring revolutionary changes in us. A similar kind of event took place in Bhaurao's life. It was an ordinary time of meals. Some guests were in the home. Arrangements for meals were in progress in the kitchen. Meanwhile Bhaurao's father was chatting with the guest.

When the guest and father sat down to eat meals, the guest casually asked, "What does your son Bhau do these days?"

"He doesn't do anything, eats two times and just loiters here and there", father replied.

"But he appears to be a healthy and a well-built young man."

"Yes that's true. That's why he does the only work of eating two times."

"Is it so?"

"Hmmm........ And he is not alone, he has a wife also." Father commented ironically.

It was at this moment, Bhaurao's wife was serving him meals. This sentence of Bhaurao's father hurt her very much. Her eyes became wet and she could not control herself. The tears rolled down from her eyes and one drop of tear fell down in a bowl of Bhaurao's dish. Bhaurao saw his weeping wife and he felt very much humiliated. He could not eat further. He felt very sad. He was insulted in the presence of the guest. His father looked at him with bulged eyes. The guest was also puzzled to see Bhaurao who got up suddenly without eating the meals and put on his clothes. He controlled his anger. His face became reddened; the effect of insult in presence of the guest was beyond tolerance for him. He thought that he must do something to give a solid answer to his father's consistent insults. He took an oath to prove himself by doing something. In a confused state of mind, he stepped out of the home and started walking like a storm. He walked towards Satara town. Koregaon to Satara was a distance of eleven to twelve miles. Bhaurao walked the distance in two hours.

He had not a single paisa in his pocket, no education, nor any support or sympathy of anyone, no food in the belly and he had turned his back to his home once and for all. What next? Where to live? What to do? How to earn the living? Plenty of questions hung in his mind. In such a dismaying state of mind, he could not realize when he reached Satara town.

Bhaurao reached Satara; he had yet not decided what to do. But he was firm about his decision. He had taken a decision not to go back to his home. He saw a ray of light even in the dense darkness. He got a way, a road to walk by. He thought what was wrong in taking tuitions of the school boys? It does not require any capital, nor any infrastructure or equipments. You do not require help of others. No risks, no loss, and no deception, nothing of the kind. This is a good business, and I can do it comfortably, he thought. You could be able to earn your own living, at the same time teaching is the noble job. Bhaurao's decision became firm. He became 'Guruji', a teacher, who had failed in the sixth standard. Bhaurao started teaching his students the subjects he failed in; English, Mathematics and Sanskrit.

The teacher must know his subjects well when he teaches. Besides, a teacher must demonstrate his subject properly. Bhaurao never liked these subjects; all of them were his enemies. His enemy number one was Sanskrit. But he had never known to accept defeat. He had never learned to withdraw. Hard work, pursuance and consistency helped him in learning the subjects. However, he had several problems with Sanskrit. He could not learn anything of Sanskrit. He understood it that he cannot learn Sanskrit without Guru's help. Giving big jerks to neck and articulating words loudly would not help him to learn Sanskrit. At last, Bhaurao found a way out. He decided to join a Sanskrit tuition. He went to meet a well known Sanskrit scholar, Pandit Gajendragadkar Shastri.

He said, "Shastriji, I have come to make a request to you."

"Tell me, what is your difficulty? I'll help you as per my capability."

"Shastriji, I wish you to teach me Sanskrit, This is my only request to you."

"But I don't have time, my boy."

"I'll come at any time you suggest. I don't have any problem of time. Tell me any convenient time you find."

"But I don't take tuitions. If you have any difficulty, you may meet me anytime."

"Shastriji, I'll have difficulties at every lesson, so I'll be coming every day."

"What do you mean?"

"Shastriji, you must be knowing Pethe, the Deputy Collector?"

"Yes, I know him; then what?"

"I am teaching his son. He is weak in Sanskrit subject."

"Oh! Is it so?"

"If you teach me Sanskrit, then only I'll be able to teach him. I am not doing anything these days than taking tuition."

"So, this is your difficulty?"

"Yes, Shastriji and I wish you to help me", Bhaurao spoke politely.

"Well, I'm ready. But for that you have to come very early in the morning at four o' clock."

"No problem Shastriji. I'll come at any time you suggest."

This was how, Bhaurao's Sanskrit tuition started at four o' clock early in the morning. He would hold a lantern in his hand and go to Shastriji's home at four in the dawn and at nine in the morning, he played the role of a teacher. He taught his student Sanskrit lessons that he had already learnt at his Guru's feet. He also taught Marathi to an English officer whose name was Pope. He was an Assistant Collector. He taught the poor students without taking fees from them. He never saw at the watch while teaching. He taught his students for three to four hours. The parents thought of him as a hard working teacher. He was taking plenty of care of his students. They thought of him as a teacher who has passion for knowledge. Bhaurao's name reached in every parts of the region as the best teacher. The number of students in his class increased rapidly. He got a name and fame as 'Patil Master' in Satara. He earned eighty rupees per month. Students in his class came from different castes, class and religion. He made no discriminations

Once, while talking about one of his Sanskrit students, Bhaurao said, "This boy is very weak in Sanskrit just as I was. I teach him Sanskrit without getting tired. But his progress in the subject is as slow as a tortoise. He does not understand his subject at all. So I have to teach him three hours in place of one hour. Even then, I do not find much progress in him. But this opportunity gave me an advantage. The boy's mother gathered up an impression about me as the best teacher. She admired me, praised me and talked about me in high sounding phrases to her neighbors."

This was how, Bhaurao got his profession. He became a student during early morning and a teacher during the rest of the day. He was a friend, philosopher and a well wisher of his students all the time.

While Bhaurao's work was in progress as a teacher, an amusing event took place. As usual, while Bhaurao was going for the Sanskrit tuition early in the morning, he heard some sound. He suddenly stopped. He guessed that someone was breaking the doors of some house. Changing his direction, he followed cautiously in the direction of the sounds he heard. He saw a thief. He was breaking doors of some house. Bhaurao was a strong man and a wrestler. He clutched him with his strong palms round his neck and hit him badly threatening, "See, if you do such things again!" The news spread across the town soon and Bhaurao's identify changed. He was now known as a 'Thieves-catching Patil-Master'!

⟨10⟩

Adversities are always the testing times. Your greatness depends upon how you encounter them. Your success, failures and your benevolence depend upon how you face them. Adversities are indeed thorny steps along with you must walk. You have an opportunity here to prove your abilities. But when you walk such a road, thorns prick you and if you don't walk, your feet burn. Great people follow such unusual paths. It is through such trials they put ideals for the people and provide the society with new ways of life.

Bhaurao confronted with such difficult times all his life. Some came in his way and some he invited. He had a testing time while he faced them. He paid a huge price. Besides, his mother too suffered enormously. She went through hard times for the sake of her son. A satanic revenge held Bhaurao for a long time and his commitment to truth was tested in this evil phenomenon. This event is known as the *Dambar Prakaran* (The Tar Scam) in Karmveer's biography

The event took place in Kolhapur during 1914. On 9 June Bhaurao received a telegram from Kolhapur. The telegram had a message: "Start immediately to Kolhapur." Kallappa Nitawe, Bhaurao's friend sent the message. Bhaurao reached Kolhapur immediately. He was disturbed. As soon as he reached the place, he asked his friend, "Why did you send the telegram?"

"Yes…Yes! Have patience! I'll tell you everything."

"Then, tell me."

"Bhau, somebody has insulted King Edwards's statue, by pasting 'tar' to his statue!"

"Oh! Then, what I have to do with it?" Bhaurao spoke annoyingly.

Nitawe whispered, "The town is tensed; the police are searching the culprit but hasn't been successful in finding any clue."

"So…, why should I worry? How am I connected to all this?" said Bhaurao.

"Yes Bhau, You're connected ….. You're connected! That's why you have been suddenly called here. People in the city and we too doubt that advocate Latthe has done this. Darbar also feels the same. We want Latthe to get into the trap."

"You do whatever you want to do. Why do you pull me in this issue?"

"It is not so Bhau. Do you remember, this same advocate Latthe expelled you from the boarding, and you had to put an end to your education? Have you forgotten all your past? This is an opportunity for you to take revenge upon Latthe. You give the witness in the court against him, and then the things will be all right."

When Bhaurao came to know all about the intrigue, he was literally shocked. He never had told lies in his life to whatsoever cause.

He said, "Look here Nitawe, Latthe teacher, whatever punishment he gave me, it was right and appropriate in its place. He never troubled me deliberately. Besides, I don't agree with you that Latthe teacher had any hand in this event. So I'll never tell lies and give false witness against him."

Nitawe's guess proved wrong. He became speechless. But he felt that he must treat Bhau differently. He took Bhaurao to his home. During night when Bhaurao was sleeping upstairs, Nitawe began to shout, "Fire .... Fire! The home is on fire!" People gathered around and the fire was extinguished immediately. Soon everything become clam and quite. Bhaurao got up from his sleep.

Nitawe said, "Bhau, you set my home on fire."

"Who? Me? How is it possible? I was sleeping upstairs."

"Who else is there in the home other than you? Besides, you've stolen my money."

"Why are you shouting? I haven't touched any of your things" Bhaurao said quietly.

"I know all that. You give witness against Latthe. Otherwise I'll inform the police tomorrow against you and the police will take your charge."

Bhaurao came to know the entire conspiracy of Nitawe. He wanted to pressurize Bhaurao and force him to give false witness in the court against Latthe. "I will never give a false witness. It is true that Latthe expelled me from the boarding but you people are expelling me from life." Bhaurao's face reddened with anger. He was utterly upset. He felt suffocated.

The next day, as Nitawe said the police came and arrested Bhaurao. He was put in the custody. His name was defamed. Bhaurao did not know what to do? How could he resolve the problem? He became numb and desperate. Several anxieties engulfed his mind. He thought to himself that there was no meaning in life. He should rather commit suicide than lead a criminal life in future. While he was going to the toilet, he got some free time from the watch of the police. There was a well near the prison. He jumped into it so that he can put an end to his life. But there was no enough water in it. He was very much disappointed for not having been successful in the suicide attempt. After a few days, he got another idea. When he got a few pieces of glasses, he crushed them and mixed in a bowl of kerosene and drank it. But, even then he could not die. He finally thought to himself that perhaps God does not want him to die. He must have been deputed to do some other work.

The news reached Koregaon. The parents came to know about his imprisonment. They became very unhappy and reached Kolhapur immediately. When they saw Bhau was trapped in a pitiable situation, they became very sad. They realized that Bhau was trapped in a very serious matter. There were several relatives of the Patil family in Kolhapur but no one came forward to help them. Every one of them turned their back and did not show any sympathy to them. Bhau's parents became helpless. They stayed in Kolhapur in a rented room and continued their efforts to free Bhau. People in Kolhapur were scared of Darbar and so they did not come forward to extend any help to them. There were several people in the town who could have extended all sort of help to Bhau's parents but because of the fear of the Darbar every one was afraid to support the truth.

The police officer Fernandes harassed Bhaurao severely. He thrashed Bhau with a whip. He tied his hands and legs and hit him every day. Bhau was a very strong man and his mind was even stronger. So he endured the police torture. But his parents were hurt when they came to know about the torture. Bhau's father had to go back to Koregaon because his official leaves were exhausted. But Bhau's mother Gangubai continued her efforts. She asked anyone whom she happened to meet:

"False allegations have put on my son and so he is in the prison. They are all false allegations. The police are thrashing him as if he is an animal. You please help me."

Then they said, "You go to so and so and he'll help you."

Mother pursued the suggestions immediately. But things did not materialize and she was disappointed. She wandered like a mad person but no one helped her. Nothing happened significant. Whatever money she had; it was all spent. She could not pay rents of the room. Kith and kins fled away. She became lonely and supportless. But Gangubai was a woman of courage. Psychologically she was very strong. She decided to do anything, at times bring the sky down but free her son at any cost.

The police at last understood that Bhaurao could not submit to their tactics. So they got scared and the case was handed over to the government. The government appointed Mr. Page, a police officer. Mr. Page was an officer of substance in such cases. He decided to take help of a low caste man. His name was Ganapat Mang. Ganapat was a well known person who gave false witnesses in the court. He was given the complete idea of what to say in the court before hand. But as he saw Bhaurao, he suddenly shouted:

"Arre ... this is our Patil Master. This man visited

our *Mangwada*, He taught our children. They became wiser because of him. This man never observed untouchability. He never charged fees for our children. Saheb, this man is our god. He is our god."

"So what? You have to give witness", the Saheb roared.

'Yes Saheb, but how can I give a false witness?'

"Ganapya", the sahib's voice was in the highest pitch. "Remember, you're speaking to me."

"Saheb, you do anything; you cut my neck, I'll not give false witness against Patil Master."

The planned scheme of the government collapsed in course of time. Gangubai met Bhaurao. She was upset on seeing Bhaurao's degrading health.

She said, "Bhau, what has happened to you? Did you give up food?"

"Aaee, I don't feel like eating; contrary, I wish to put an end to my life."

"My boy, don't say that", said mother, tears rolling from her eyes.

"Don't give up, don't get disheartened. Nothing will happen to us. We haven't done anything wrong to anyone in our life."

"Aaee, then why these allegations? How god can be so cruel?"

Bhaurao's eyes became wet. His heart heaved in tears. Mother caressed him; she fondled his back with love. She said, "Bhau, god knows everything. He is not cruel as you think. You will be free. I am with you. But you have to eat. You have to follow me."

"Yes, Aaee. I'll do what you say. I'll eat. Is that all right now?"

Gangubai met police inspector and got permission to provide Bhau with food that she cooked. She visited the prison everyday with tiffin for Bhau. Within a few days adversities increased. All money that she had was spent, she become supportless. Nobody gave her things on credit. She was with her two kids. At last, she worked as a labourer at an inn and baked *bhakaris* every day. What else a poor mother could do? She was getting some Jawar dough as remuneration towards her work.

A case was filed as Bhaurao had made an attempt of suicide. Subsequently, the imprisonment was increased by six months. Still Gangubai was not disheartened. She decided to meet the Maharaj. It was not a simple thing then to meet the Maharaj. He was always escorted by the police. There was police force deputed while the Maharaj was on visits.

The *baggi* of Maharaja started moving. On both sides of the road, there was a crowd of people to greet him. Gangubai was in the crowd. She suddenly came out of the crowd. She went towards the baggi and bowed down on seeing the Maharaj.

She said, "Maharaja, I'm your sister. I wish to make you a request."

"Yes, tell me what is your difficulty?"

The baggi had almost stopped now. "Maharaja, my son, Bhau is in the prison. He is innocent. He is wrongly punished. You make inquiry. He has not done anything wrong. Please help me to release him from the prison."

"Yes, Yes! I will make inquiry. You take food. Stay at our palace."

The Maharaja made inquiry and he came to know that Gangubai was Jain by caste. He made arrangements to provide her with necessary food items at her place with a message that she should not worry about her son and he would personally look into the matter to help her. The kind words of the Maharaja provided both mother and son hopes of an early release. They became happy.

A month passed in between but nothing significant happened. Gangubai met the Maharaja again. He sent her to advocate Ghatage. The advocate made an appeal in the court. The appeal was unattended for some time. Meanwhile, Gangubai was pressurized to give a false witness in the court. She was given bribe.

Gangubai refused it and said angrily, "I've four sons. I'll suppose that one of my sons is no more. But I'll never follow your wrong paths." She threatened them that things will be worse if they approach her again. When they saw anger of mother, they never turned their evil faces to her.

The court at last issued the order of Bhau's release. Bhaurao's father from Koregaon was also trying hard for his son's release. The Collector of Satara wrote a letter to an officer in Kolhapur; he was an Englishman. The letter played an important role in this respect.

Bhau's parents were waiting for their son at the prison doors. They were eager to meet him. But the police were not ready to release him. They were finding some reasons to withhold him in the prison. The parents applied to the British Regiment and reported about the eccentric behaviour of the police. Thus, Bhaurao was finally released. Even then, the police chased them up to the railway station, but they could not do anything as they had no warrant with them. Besides, Bhau's father lodged a complaint against them at the railway police station. Thus, Bhaurao left for Vita along with his parents because his father was transferred from Koregaon to Vita.

11

Kolhapur offered Bhaurao life of luxury in the Maharaja's palace. The same Kolhapur offered him the prison. Kolhapur gave him delicious food, but the same Kolhapur gave him the police atrocities. The Kolhapur event taught him several things. He learnt that truth always excels; mother's love is a great power. A common person like Ganapat Mang possesses power of humanism but a so called friend like Nitwe lacks it. When disasters and adversaries follow you one by one, your so called kith and kin flee away one by one from you. You have to wait for justice at god's house but you always get justice in god's house. Bhaurao learnt these and many more things through the perilous Kolhapur event. Things which he could never have learnt in the school text-books, he learnt them in the open school of life. Experience taught him several things. He realized that the experiences you face in an open school of life become your true teacher, a true-guru. Such experiences build wisdom in you and at times, shape and mend you also.

After great suffering, Bhaurao thought of nothing but rest. And then he again went out in search of some work. In the first place, he was an elderly person in the home. His father gradually lost hearing powers and so he resigned his job. Naturally, the entire responsibility of the family fell on Bhaurao's shoulder. He could not resume his tuition work in Satara. So he began to work with his classmate Atamarampant Ogale. Mr. Ogale had opened a glass industry. He invited Bhaurao to join the company. His work was to advertise the glass products and increase the sale of the company. Bhaurao had already some experience as an Insurance Agent. It helped him to become a successful salesman. Because of his hard work, the sale of the company products increased. As a result, it helped him to obtain some hike in his monthly income. Honesty, hard work and sustenance of Bhaurao took the company to a substantial height.

Bhaurao's qualifications as a salesman attracted attention of Laxamnrao Kirloskar, a well established industrialist of the time. The glass industry of Ogale was previously located in Kirloskarwadi. When a well known industrialist invited Bhaurao, Ogale appreciated it and did not take any objection to it. He allowed Bhaurao to join the Kirloskar Company. Kirloskar offered Bhaurao more salary. The Kirloskar Company products were useful for the agricultural business. They were made from iron. The Company had produced an iron plough for the first time. Previously, the farming plough was made from wood. The customers of the Company products were obviously the farming communities of the region. Bhaurao settled down with his family for some time at Kundal during this period. He was now very much engrossed in his work. The sale of the Kirloskar products increased because of his hard work. Bhaurao would forget everything while he was occupied in his work. He persuaded farmers, agents and merchants to prefer the iron plough. He convinced his customers the usefulness of the product. On several occasions, he demonstrated how to use the plough. These efforts of Bhaurao made Laxamnrao Kirloskar very happy. His monthly salary went on increasing in course of time. Bhaurao's salary reached the scale of ninety rupees per month. It was a pretty big amount in those days. You could speculate it very easily. Then, ten gram gold was sold for twenty rupees and the cost of one sack of Jawar was just four rupees. Five rupees was enough for monthly expenses of a family then, if a family is considered as consisting of five persons. Bhaurao's financial status improved. Besides, his wife was not a spendthrift person. She was, on the other hand, very arduous and upright. She did not spend money on unnecessary articles. Therefore, Bhaurao was able to achieve progress rapidly in several contexts.

The people in the industry then did not observe the caste discriminations outside the home. They respected everyone though they belonged to different castes. Bhaurao was Jain by caste but he visited workers' homes though they were low caste people. The factory had a cricket team and Bhaurao was the team manager. He would for example sell tickets of a charity show and extend all sorts of help. Sometimes, he went for hunting or on some occasions, he worked as a guard during the night to protect the surrounding campus from thieves and robbers.

During this period, Laxmibai started suffering from the stomach problems. The doctor advised for an operation but she was not ready for it. Radhabai Kirloskar prepared her mind for the operation. Laxmibai was operated successfully at the Mission Hospital in Miraj. Now Bhaurao's life was settled down; it was going on smoothly. Bhaurao got the work he liked, the work of common farmers. He got the work to establish meaningful rapport with the farming community of our country.

12

Bhaurao wandered extensively as a salesman. He saw common peoples' life closely, the life of Bahujan Samaj. He had a true *darshan* of the real Indian life. He saw that villagers were very naïve people. They were illiterate and backward. They had no sense of how they were consistently and systematically exploited. Ignorance, blind faith and superstitious had engulfed them. They were exploited in the name of religion. The social evils like cast discriminations and untouchability had surrounded them. The poor and the landless were somehow struggling to survive helplessly. Untouchables and women were treated like animals. They were the worst victims of the evil system. Numerous evil customs were uprooting man. He was living an enslaved life in such a whirlwind of evil drama. How can we free them from such perilous punishments? How could we prevent them from exploitation? How could we eradicate blind faith? These and such other questions pestered Bhaurao. He developed a deep sense of affinity towards the people. He thought that he must do something for them. This thought consistently troubled his mind. He could not find peace of mind. He became restless. At last, he discovered the only remedy on this predicament of the people and it was education. We must educate people properly and we have to create awareness among them to end social evils. They must stand on their own feet. They must become independent economically. They should voice against exploitation and enslavement. Light of knowledge only could help them to put an end to darkness of ignorance that has engulfed them. Bhaurao got a pathway. He got his remedy and at once he began his missionary work.

He visited Dudhagaon village frequently. It was located in Sangli district. With the help of a few friends, he started a *Mandal* for the spread of education among the bahujan communities at Dudhagaon. The Mandal started a boarding at Dudhagaon. About 50 boys from different castes and creed came to the boarding. The boys were encouraged to carry out their regular studies. They were provided with necessary materials; for example oil-lamps during the night time. Then, the electricity facility was not available. Boarding facilities and facilities of physical exercises were provided to them.

During harvest times, Bhaurao visited farm sites

and request people: "You give money for oil to cook food. You give me chilies from your farm for boys and you give me grains for boys." Farmers wholeheartedly gave Bhaurao whatever he demanded. There was a teacher. His name was Madhvanna. He helped Bhaurao and shouldered the responsibility. But in course of time, the teacher was transferred. Bhaurao left the factory and the boarding work subsequently lost its usual speed.

But his passion for propagation of education made him impatient and prevented him from doing anything. He started a boarding at Nerle in Walwa tehsil in 1921. The district collector, an Englishman Mayes came to inaugurate the boarding. He admired Bhaurao's attempts of starting a boarding in unfavourable situation. With the establishment of the boarding, Bhaurao did two things: first, he went to each home and asked for a fistful of grain.

Observe the following conversation that Bhaurao did while asking for a fistful of grain at each door, usually with woman of the home:

"My Sister, don't you grind grain everyday for your home?"

"Yes, baba, one has to do it."

"If we don't do it, how can we feed our children?"

"Yes sister. I too have many children from the neighboring region of this village, they have come for education. They are very poor. Do you know anything about this?"

"Yes baba, we have heard about it. This is a good thing. The poor will learn a few things."

"Then sister, you must give something for them."

"What can I give you? I have not a single paisa to spend on my children."

"Sister, don't give me money. When you sit down to grind grain, you may give a fistful of grain and nothing else. You may drop the grain in this sack."

"Is that so? Then it is not a difficult thing. Nobody will remain hungry in my home if I give a fistful of grain for your children."

And then, Bhaurao gave her a sack and sister hung it at the grinding tool. She dropped a fistful of grain in the sack regularly. Bhaurao's children collected the sacks from every home weekly and the poor children made arrangements for their daily bread. A fistful of grain was not a heavy donation for the poor. This fistful of grain was a great donation of the poor for the poor. It was a positive support of the poor for the poor.

Secondly, a small amount of donation in the form of money that Bhaurao collected from the tillers' taxes was also tolerable. Such attempts of Bhaurao helped the poor farmers to learn a new thing. They understood the importance of education and they developed positive attitudes towards education. Besides, such donations for the education of the poor produced awareness among the poor that every one of them is connected to the community at large and it is everybody's social responsibility to provide a helping hand in education as a social organization. Bhaurao showed that such small donation for the cause of education from the poor was not a heavy burden. He developed an attitude among the poor that they must do something for the society. Bhaurao inculcated a feeling of social commitment among the people and it was an important development in the work that Bhaurao was going to begin in near future.

⟨13⟩

The progressive thoughts of Shahu Maharaj had introduced Bhaurao Mahatma Phule's ideology. Phule's works had left a deep impression on his mind. He was under Phule's influence so much so that he even acted an important role in the film produced on the life and works of Mahatma Phule. The Satyashodhak Movement of Mahatma Phule was in full swing in those days in Maharahtra. Shahu Maharaj had provided a solid basis and support to the movement. The activists of the movement visited villages and interior regions of Maharashtra. They organized meetings and conferences and enlightened the public. The activists also organized cultural programmes like *Jalase* in which *Vag, Lavani* were presented to attract the public. Bhaurao participated in such programmes. Jalase showed how the priest class exploited the poor and the money lenders (*Savakars*) harassed the poor. The programmes followed meetings where speeches were delivered to enlighten upon Phule's ideas. Bhaurao participated in such activities and he did his job sincerely. He delivered speeches and presented Phule's ideas. He made a plea to the people to educate their boys and girls, peasants and working classes. He told them to stop caste discriminations and untouchability. He persuaded them not to worship and conduct Puja of *stones*. He requested the people not to give any *daan* and *dakshina* (money or gift) to the priests. He also told them not to get indulged in habit of drinking wine, not to go for any loan. On the contrary, he strongly advised them to follow a path of education. These and such other were the enlightening thoughts and advice that Bhaurao propagated through the Satyashodhak programmes.

Once, Shahu Maharaj was going to attend a Jalasa programme at Lohgaon, near Pune. A huge crowd was curious enough to have a glance at the Maharaja. At a critical moment of the opening of the programme, the *Dholakiwala* was missing. He was looked for here and there but he was not found anywhere. A problem rose up as to who will play the *dholak*? How the programme will start? Bhaurao came forward and said, "Is that the problem? I'll play the dholak. I will do it as much as I could but your show must go." And the programme went on. Bhaurao was thus discovered as a dholak player. Bhaurao had often sung ballads based on the themes of social reformation. Once he struck the *duff* (a musical instrument) the crowd listened to him with their heart throbbing in sensations. The huge mountain like voice of Bhaurao exploded and the crowd became spellbound. It listened to him with a heart in their ears. Bhaurao's emphasis was on action and participation rather that just deliver speeches. This was how he pursued Mahatma Phule's ideology and methodology. He decided to put an end to the casteial, religious and class discriminations. If we are born as human beings; then why these differences? Bhaurao did not approve of the ideology of superiority and inferiority.

Once, he visited Sajjangad where on *Dasnavami* a huge religious festival was in progress. He had a good number of Satyashodhak activists with him. There was a huge gathering of devotees. Devotees recited Ramdas

Swami's poems and *slokas* in a loud choir. They distributed Ghee-Prasad. Other sweets were also given as *Prasad* to the devotees. The crowd of devotees was jostling to get the Prasad.

Bhaurao requested the organizers. "Is this *Prasad* given for all devotees?"

"Of course, we give Prasad to devotees as a full meal." Someone said.

"The devotees must be giving grains and donations for the Prasad."

"The devotees of Samarth Ramdas Swami donate as per their capacity. The entire community gives a helping hand"

"The common man of the society is a part of god, and then all people must get Prasad at one time," Bhaurao said sternly.

"How is it possible? First the Brahmins and then the other castes." One devotee said.

"Why?" Bhaurao asked as if he hadn't understood anything.

"The Brahmin is the most superior to all and obviously he gets the first right."

Bhaurao became furious; he could not control his wrath. He spoke in a high pitch sound,

"This will not do here afterwards. All people must get Prasad at one time only.".

"We cannot go against religion and traditions prevalent since long time", someone said in the same tone and pitch of Bhaurao.

"Let the religion go into ditch. Is this practice called religion?" Bhaurao lost his temper.

"Hold your tongue; otherwise you will not get the Prasad."

"I'll see how I don't get it. We're all children of god; god belongs to all. You accept grains and donation from all, then, why do you make discriminations between 'these people' and 'those people'?"

"We don't do that, it is religion and culture which have brought up these things. And let me ask you, who're you to raise these questions?", asked one of the priests.

One word led to another and it resulted into a big quarrel. The people got huddled. Most of them were in favour of Bhaurao. In the beginning, it was only a word war but gradually, it developed into a serious matter and later on it burst into a riot. As a result, the festival place turned into a battlefield. The people had to leave the place without taking Prasad. This was Bhaurao's first attempt of establishing the principles of equality and humanism.

Bhaurao then turned to Audumbar. It is a famous place where a shrine of Datta God is located. It is situated on the banks of the Krishna River. It is nearer to Bhilawadi village. During the festival time, the devotees were treated in the same way. Discriminations were made on the basis of cast and creed. This time, Bhaurao played a trick. He started a corner meeting at a place where the high cast devotees were taking Prasad. Thousands of people attended the meeting. Naturally, the distribution activity of the Prasad came to a standstill. The Prasad was prepared from grains donated by the devotees. Bhaurao started distributing the Prasad. One of the priests threatened him not to touch the Prasad. Finally, Bhaurao prepared the food and asked the people belonging to different castes to take the Prasad. He also requested the Brahmins to take the Prasad. He requested people from all castes to sit together and eat the Prasad. The Prasad is not for any one person or a particular community, he said. He told them that they had to wait for some time. The topsy-turvy event shocked the Brahmins who were in the habit of eating the Prasad at the first round. They were very much disturbed and left the place without eating the Prasad. While leaving the place, they abused Bhaurao and his people. This was the second victory that Bhaurao won in the campus of a temple.

This event took place in the year 1920-21. Mahatma Gandhiji was trying to say the same thing during the period. He was pressing for the demand of native commodities that is Swadeshi. He had organized a protest movement on the welcome ceremony of Prince of Wales and he made an appeal to the people not to participate in the event. Gandhiji organized a protest movement in Bombay.

Gandhiji made a strong plea for the use of Swadeshi clothes. He organized a number of programmes at different places where he persuaded people to burn foreign clothes. The bonfires of foreign clothes brought about a transformation in the ideology of Bhaurao. He followed Ghandhiji's principles of simplicity and wore a Dhoti and a white Gandhi cap. He took a pledge in the light of the bonfire of the foreign clothes that he will never use foreign clothes. He kept his words till his death. After 1930, he stopped using the cap and shoes also. In 1945 in the scorching heat of April with his student P. G. Patil, he walked the Bombay tar roads without shoes. But Bhaurao took care of his student; he did not allow his student to walk without shoes.

14

Bhaurao became a well known speaker of the Satyashodhak Movement in Maharashtra. His impact as a speaker grew significantly. The main theme of his speeches was sympathy towards the poor and anger against exploitation and social injustice. He attacked the rich money lenders who took the disadvantage of the illiterate ignorant poor. Bhaurao thought that service to the poor was service to the society. So, he put more emphasis on education of the poor. He put his fingers categorically on the indiscriminations and unequal treatment given to the poor. He saw that his speeches attracted crowds. People were convinced in what he was saying. But there were no significant changes in the society. He realized that only delivering speeches was useless. People listened to the speaker and forgot about what he said within a couple of hours. He thought that slogans do not change people; the society must change from within. What can we do then? We have to destroy economic and religious slavery. People are psychologically handicapped. There is a casteial structure and we have to destroy it. This is possible only when we educate people properly. Bhaurao thought that if you want to put an end to social ills and evils, the most powerful tool of social change is only education. He thought to himself that this was only the weapon that could help him. It will enable him to fight on a number of fronts. So, he decided to do some fundamental work in the field of education and concentrate on a single programme, instead of wasting his energy on delivering speeches.

In 1919, a meeting of the Satyashodhak Samaj was organized at Kale, near Karad town. Keshwarao Bagwe presided over the meeting. Bhaurao attended the meeting. He spoke in the meeting. He said, "We are trying to propagate our ideas and thoughts through meetings, Jalases and such programmes. We are not lacking in our sincere efforts but still there are no changes in the society that we are looking forward to. I do not see any alternative than education in this context. I therefore think that we must start an educational institution to educate the bahujan communities." Bhaurao's suggestion was granted and at last an educational institution namely *Rayat Shikshan Sanstha* came into existence to provide with free education to the poor. The purpose of the Sanstha was to encourage respect and love towards education, to establish fraternity and solidarity among all castes, to make students industrious and economically independent. With the help of the people of Kale, a boarding at Kale was started. The boys at the boarding earned their living. They bought their clothes and books with their own earnings. The people gave them grains. These were the first official attempts of the beginning of Rayat Shikshan Sanstha. Bhaurao visited the boarding whenever he got free time. He was then serving in Kirloskar Factory as a salesman. He felt very unhappy because he did not find enough time to look after the boarding work. Later, he decided that he must work as a full time activist for the cause of education. So, he thought of resigning his job. He met Laxamnrao Kirloskar with the application letter to resign his job.

"I have come to you to request you."

"Yes, any problem Bhaurao in your work?"

"No...no... not at all. There is no problem. I have an altogether different problem."

"Don't get embarrassed. Tell me Bhaurao without hesitation. As there is increase in the sale of the factory products, do you want a hike in your salary?", asked Laxamanrao.

"No...not at all. That's not the problem. But... but I've decided to resign the job."

"What? You wish to resign? This is not good Bhaurao. You have good salary and if you wish, I'll increase your salary. You don't take such a decision."

"Laxamnrao, I wish to do my social and educational work which I love more than anything else and for which I need more free time." Bhaurao opened his mind.

Kirloskar said, "Bhaurao, you can do your social and educational work by doing our job and which you are already doing. We never had any difficulties and we'll never bring any problem in your favorite work."

But Bhaurao did not take Kirloskar's advice seriously. He submitted the resignation to him and Laxamanrao's respect for Bhaurao was not affected. For he knew well his contributions rendered for his company. Bhaurao attended Silver Jubilee Function of the company deliberately to show his respect towards the Kirloskars. He declared on this occasion to start a school at Kirloskarwadi.

The resignation of the Kirloskar Company offered Bhaurao ample time for the social work. At this turn of time, Dhanjeesha Kapur had started a factory manufacturing iron material at Padali Station. He was looking for a man who knew all operations and other things of the factory. He came to Bhaurao to ask for his help.

Bhaurao said, "I'm busy with my education work, so I don't wish to do any other job." Kapur was a very sharp and practical-minded man. He tempted Bhaurao, "See Bhaurao, you help my factory and I'll help your educational institution. We both will have a mutual advantage in this enterprise." Bhaurao needed financial help and so he could not say no to Kapur.

He said, "I'll help you in getting your factory settled down. But you'll keep some profit from the factory income for the benefit of the education of the poor and this financial help will continue as long as the factory will exist." Kapur agreed to the proposal.

Bhaurao called his friends and activists who were involved in such jobs and helped Kapur to start the factory. The factory started manufacturing its products. He also got good market for his products. The factory flourished and started getting good profit. The Kirloskar iron plough and Kapur iron plough come into the market which provided an advantage to the farmer. Because of the competition in the market, the price of the plough came down.

Kapur did not keep his word. Bhaurao reminded him that he had given him a word to provide him with financial help for the education of the poor. He pursued his demand for a long time but on every occasion Kapur somehow postponed his decision.

Bhaurao realized that it was useless to meet Kapur. He realized that he will not help him in any condition. At last, he decided to do something and take a final decision in this respect.

So he finally met Kapur and asked him, "Why are you not keeping your words? You promised me to help, give me money from the factory profit for the boarding? Why don't you help me? What's your problem?"

"What promises you are talking about? I don't remember anything that I gave you any promises,"

Kapur pretended and wore a mask on his face.

"You promised me Mr. Kapur to help me from the profit of the factory." Bhaurao reminded Kapur.

"Do you say so? I promised you? It's possible!" Kapur said.

"You did promise Mr. Kapur! I therefore worked night and day and this factory was raised and within a year's period! It gives you huge profits today." Bhaurao's anger was rising gradually and it is very difficult to control him if his wrath explodes against anyone.

"It's possible Bhaurao that I must have given you word that you are talking about but that's not possible for me now."

Kapur expressed his inability to help Bhaurao in an irresponsible tone. He took Bhaurao's words very casually. Bhaurao was now sure that Kapur was interested only in money and not in helping the poor. He lost his temper and picked up a rifle. But it was the timely advice of Prabodhankar Thakare who persuaded him that the factory owners cannot have love for the poor. Thus, Bhaurao escaped an impending disaster. It was an invitation for his own destruction.

Thakare said, "What are you doing Bhaurao? What advantage you are going to get through such an act? Don't behave like a mad person. You first cool down. If you want to do something for the poor, you must work by yourself. How the factory owners will have pity for the poor?". Thakare took Bhaurao to his home and cooled him down and thus an unwanted menace was avoided.

Bhaurao learnt a lesson from this experience. If you wish to do something and achieve what you are looking for, you have to do it by yourself. Those who depend on others, they never succeed in achieving what they aim at. They usually become failures.

$$\langle 15 \rangle$$

Bhaurao gave up hopes that Kapur might provide him financial help. He decided to devote his entire life for the Sanstha. That way, he had already started working for the Sanstha by establishing a boarding for the poor boys in 1919 at Kale.

In 1924, he started a boarding for the Harijan at Satara. He had resigned his job. Kapur had deceived him, so there was not a penny in the home. In such a poor situation, he brought one Harijan student with him. He stayed with him in his home. One more Harijan boy was added. Thus, the number went on multiplying. When it became impossible for him to accommodate all boys, he made separate arrangements for them at a an inn. Bhaurao paid bills of the inn. He asked for financial help from his friends. Later on, each boy lived at different homes of his friends. Some of his friends agreed to pay monthly expenses of a few boys. Even then, it was very difficult for him to manage the expenses. There were a few friends of him to provide help and support but there were many at the other end. So what to do in such a situation? Laxmibai had golden ornaments. They weighed about 800 grams. One by one, she sold them to meet the boarding expenses. The boarding boys therefore called Laxmibai *Vahini* and Bhaurao *Anna*. They were like parents to them.

Bhaurao had many problems so as to run the boarding facilities. Several of them came from backward communities and some of them were Muslims. The Maratha boys had a privilege to dine inside the inn but the backward and Muslim boys had to take their food in the courtyard or outside premises of the Inn. Bhaurao tolerated such arrangements, though he did not approve of them. He made separate arrangements at different places. He got up very early in the morning with a lantern in his hand. He looked after boys personally and resolved their difficulties. He set his sharp eyes on their studies. He had hard tasks to perform. He had a dream; he had a vision to produce ideal citizens for welfare of the society. He wanted to liberate men and women who were clutched in slumber of ignorance and darkness for centuries and centuries.

Bhaurao played several tactics to get hold of new boys for his boarding. Students who were appearing for the seventh standard final written examination had to come to Satara. He provided them with boarding facilities. He offered them food. Sometimes, he arranged wrestling contests and informed them about his works. Besides, he visited interior regions of the district to tap the rural talent. Barrister P.G. Patil, a village lad that Bhaurao tapped was from Kawalapur village of Sangli district. While crossing a local water stream, he shouldered the tiny-little lad who later excelled all academic records of Bombay University. Bhaurao sent him abroad for his advanced education. He rose up as one of the major Indian educationists and held many prestigious posts like Vice-Chancellors of Shivaji University and later on the Chairman of MPSC (Maharashtra Public Service Commission).

Parents felt awkward in the initial stages. The parents of *Savarna* communities for example Marathas were reluctant to send their children to the boarding. They felt that if their children take education with untouchables, their community will excommunicate them. Bhaurao convinced them that nothing of the sort will happen. He said that let people talk anything. You cannot control them. What is important is to educate the children.

Boys belonging to several communities lived together in the boarding. They did all sorts of work together. They cooked and studied together. The boys consisted of varied castes and religions. People hushed them up when they went for bathing at public tanks. The boys had to visit the public tanks because the bathing facilities were absent nearby.

A man from municipality opposed them to bathe at a public place. They were discouraged and so they often became embittered. Some of them did not pay any attention to such trifles. They unhesitatingly bathed at such places. They washed their clothes too and so it often triggered bitter quarrels between people and the boys. There were several such problems and they went on increasing. The barbers of Satara town were reluctant to cut hairs of the boarding boys because they knew that Bhaurao's boys did not follow caste discriminations. So a new problem erupted as to who will cut the hairs of the boys. Bhaurao gave a thought to it and found out a good solution. There was a barber boy in the boarding. He bought necessary saloon tools and the barber boy cut hairs of boys in the boarding itself.

The barber boy got a professional training in the boarding itself without extra efforts. The backward boys of the boarding enabled to avoid insults and humiliation of the public. The money was saved. Boys got a lesson of self-help. Bhaurao thus taught boys new ways of living. Let come difficulties and disasters, you can always overcome them by self-help. Such lessons enabled boys to become courageous enough and live a life of dignity.

Harijan boys often complained to Bhaurao that other boys made fun of them. They were ridiculed for their rural dialect and intonation. Sometimes the teachers also insulted them. Bhaurao told them to neglect such things. Besides, he told them to take more interest in their studies. He occasionally visited the schools and helped his boys. On different festive occasions, discriminations were done in the schools. Backward and Harijans were kept outside the school. The boys of Bhaurao opposed such customs based on casteial discriminations. Plenty of conflicts took place. Bhaurao told boys to face things fearlessly and live with dignity. The boys went through thick and thin. Such disasters made them rough and tough. Later, they grew into recognized personalities with robust rural physique and iron like solid minds. The collective strength of such boys made the opposition of the orthodox communities ineffective.

16

$\mathbf{P}$eople gradually realized the importance of English education. Parents therefore sent their children to Bhaurao's boarding. The number increased in the boarding. It became difficult now for Bhaurao to accommodate boys in rented places. A separate independent and larger place was necessary to accommodate them at one place. Bhaurao got such a place in 1927. The Maharaja of Satara donated him a place. It was called Dhanini's Baug. This was a garden place used by the royal women from the family of the Maharaja of Satara. Bhaurao shifted his boarding in the garden place. The boys cleaned the place and built huts on a ten acre land. They tilled the land. They got sufficient work. Self-help, co-operation, simplicity and imaginative insight enabled Bhaurao to build up a brave new world. The collective efforts produced an entirely different world that Bhaurao was looking forward to. There were two wells in the garden. So there was sufficient water supply at the place. Fully grown up trees like coconut, mango, tamarind already existed. The land was fertile. The boarding life flowered in the companionship of nature. A new life initiated just like that of Tagore's Shantiniketan.

Mahatma Gandhi was then touring Bombay State. Bhaurao's boarding was acquiring name and fame. He had an intense wish that his boys must shine in studies and acquire meritorious success in schools. But because of the funding problems, he did not want his boys to suffer. He therefore collected donations. He spent money from his pocket. From 1924 to 1927, he collected donations worth rupees one hundred and sixty three only but he spent about six thousand rupees from his personal resources.

Bhaurao intensely wished that Mahatma Gandhi must pay a visit to his boarding. So he wrote a letter to him. Gandhi wrote him back. He informed him that he was willing to visit his boarding. On the receipt of the letter, Bhaurao immediately started preparing for his visit. Cleaning, road making in the boarding premises began. He wanted to name his boarding as Rajarshi Shahu Maharaj Boarding because he got the inspiration of education work from him. He even prepared a hoarding made from a piece of cloth bearing the name of Shahu Boarding House. But suddenly something went wrong. Somebody misreported Gandhi. He was told that

Bhaurao's work was not worth visiting and Gandhi sent a message to Bhaurao that because of short of time he was unable to pay a visit to his boarding.

Bhaurao was upset. The boys too were disheartened. But Bhaurao did not lose his heart. He learnt the real tug behind the whole conspiracy. He decided to go forward. He took his boarding boys and came on the road where Mahatma Gandhi was to enter the town. He politely asked Gandhi why he cancelled his visit to his boarding. Upon this Gandhi looked at his personal secretary, Mahadev Bhai and he looked in turn to the local leader. A leader at last said that Bhaurao's work is not so worth visiting.

On which Bhaurao said, "I give education to boys of all castes including boys from the backward communities. I even provide them food and look after them like their parents." Gandhiji was shocked when he came to know about the boarding of Bhaurao. He asked Bhaurao, "Boys of all castes and creed live together? What do you say?"

Gandhi sternly told the local leader to take the car to the boarding. The local leader subsequently took the car to the boarding. The leader was obviously humiliated. The boys become very happy when they saw Gandhiji in their boarding premises. The news spread in the town like a wild wind. Bapuji inaugurated the boarding. It was now called Rajarshi Shahu Boarding House. "How much money did Maharaj give you?" asked Gandhiji out of curiosity. Bhaurao said "Not a single paisa!" Gandhi was surprised to know it.

A Harijan student namely Dnyandev Gholap delivered an introductory speech and informed Gandhi how Bhaurao established the boarding. He reported caste-wise names of the boys. Then Bhaurao introduced boys of the boarding. Knowing upon a Mang student namely Laxman Babaji Bhingardev who achieved the first prize in Sanskrit, Mahatma was excited. He took out the garland from his neck and put it around the boy and said that the boy deserved it more than him.

Bhaurao reported Bapuji that the boys of all castes live together in his boarding. They work together and dine together. They take education through self-help. Gandhi was overwhelmed to know it. He said, "I too tried to do this experiment at Sabarmati but could not succeed in it. Bhaurao, you have done this experiment successfully which I always longed for. I give you credit for this and my best wishes are always with you for your future success. You are producing a new society, a new culture here. I'll give you all possible help. My blessings are with you."

Gandhi sent five hundred rupees as grants from Harijan Seva Sangh for Bhaurao's boarding. He realized the significance of his work. He always had a close watch on his work since his visit to the boarding. Bhaurao met Gandhi whenever it was possible for him. Once, Gandhiji came to Panchgani for rest. Bhaurao met him. Gandhiji made inquiries about his work and told Bhaurao to pursue his work with devotion and speed. He admired Bhaurao's work and said that his service itself was a true image of his work. After the assassination of Gandhi in a meeting at Satara, Bhaurao declared that he will start 101 High Schools in the name of Mahatma Gandhi. He fulfilled his pledge in the following next six to seven years.

Knowing that Gandhiji is providing grants to Bhaurao's Boarding, Bombay Government showed willingness to provide grants with a condition that Bhaurao should not accept Gandhiji's grants. But Bhaurao wrote to the Government and told that he will continue to receive grants from Gandhiji and if the Government wants to provide grants for the boarding in spite of Gandhiji's grants, he will be happy to receive the government grants. On the other hand, if the government wants him to stop Gandhiji's grants; he wrote to the government that he would rather prefer Gandhiji's grants to the government grants. Finally, the government considered the significance of Bhaurao's work and provided five hundred rupees as annual grants to the boarding.

The boarding was now shifted to Dhanini's Baug, a separate place for his boarding.

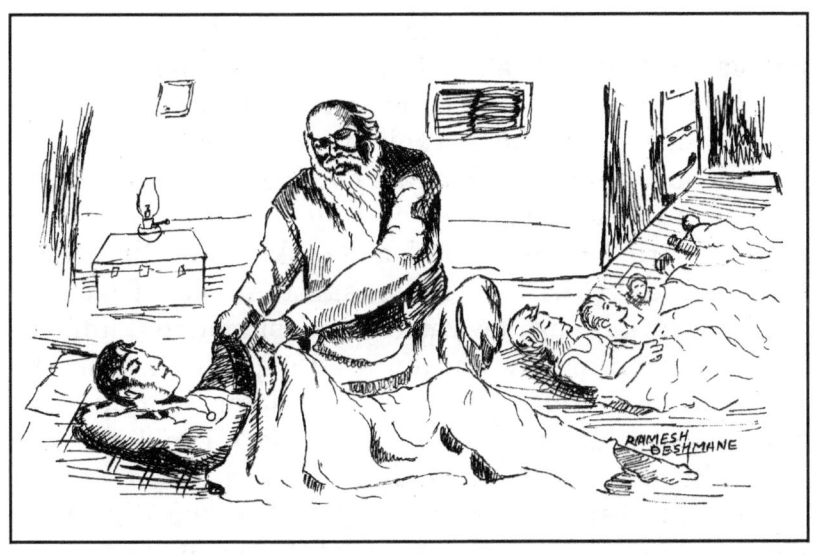

Therefore it became convenient to him to monitor boys and do a number of experiments. He carried on different activities. He woke up the boys at 4:30 am. The Morning Prayers would be conducted so early. After the prayer, boys worked for an hour. The breakfast would be served and then the boys would study and after meals they attended their respective schools. During evening, they played and after dinner they again did their regular school home work.

Bhaurao himself delivered speeches on many occasions. He often encouraged them to play native games. He provided them training in Indian games like wrestling and mallakhamb. He gave them books on different subjects. There were contests conducted among boys like elocution, games, vegetable productions, etc.

Bhaurao was usually on the tour for collecting funds and hunting rural talents. In his absence, his wife, Laxmibai looked after the boarding. She took care of boys in every possible way. Then let it be any work from cooking to anything else till boys go to bed. When there might be funding problem, she handled it in a confident way. At times, she sold her golden ornaments but was particular that boys should not remain hungry.

Bhaurao was a true educationist. He had a close eye on aptitudes of his boys, their likes and dislikes. There was a boy namely Bhingardev. He had passionate interest in Sanskrit. Bhaurao sent him to Wai, a town near Satara where he had a Sanskrit Pandit friend, namely Tarkthirtha Laxamshastri Joshi. Teaching Bhingardev a Mang, low-caste boy, Joshi found it difficult in the beginning. He encountered opposition from the Brahmin community. But he did not deter from his work and taught Bhingardev Sanskrit unhesitatingly.

There were Middle-School and High-School scholarship exams in those days. The boarding boys appeared for the exams. Several of them were successful and claimed scholarships. Similarly, boys participated in sports in the town organized by different schools and won many medals. Bhaurao's boys were rural and they had good physical built up. They easily won such contests. Besides, their work at the boarding was not affected due to such extra-curricular activities. On the other hand, they marshaled extra energy from such contests and they pursued the boarding work with more enthusiasm.

The new place, Dhanini's Baug had plenty of land. There were also two big wells, so there was no scarcity of water. They used the land for agricultural purpose. The boys grew grains and vegetables in the land. Coconut trees gave coconuts, banana trees banana. The only scarcity was that of milk. Bhaurao purchased four buffaloes for milk. He also purchased four oxen for ploughing the land. In the beginning, a *mot* came and then an engine. The boys did all sorts of agricultural work. They drove mot to irrigate the land, plantation for vegetables, remove weeding and winnowing work. Contests were conducted for getting more and more agricultural produce among the boys. This was how, the boarding started getting good income through the agricultural produce. The cattle also got fodder. The boys looked after the cattle. They washed them, fed them and milked them. They took vegetables in the market. The people preferred the boarding vegetables because they were of good quality than the vegetables sold in the market.

Bhaurao paid regular visits to the schools that his boys attended. He made inquiries about their progress. If his boys were found bunking classes, not attempting the home work, he took them to task. If they did not obey him, they were punished. Such boys were given extra work in the field. He announced punishments so that the rest of boys came to know about them. That was how to avoid humiliation the boys obeyed Bhaurao's orders. Similarly, he admired boys who obtained scholarship and achieved good grades in examinations. It encouraged them to study more and go for good grades in exams. The school headmasters were happy with the boarding boys.

Discipline was observed meticulously in the boarding. The boys were not allowed to grow their hair;

visiting hotel was considered as a bad habit, the idea of eating pan, tobacco chewing, smoking biddies or cigarettes was beyond imagination. The boys usually did not press their clothes. Their possessions were a few things like a blanket, a dish, a bowl and two to three sets of dress. They built a thatched hut and kept it clean by applying cow-dung to it. They washed their clothes and dishes, bowls and plates. The lesson in the dignity of labour was effortlessly percolated through labour and hard work that they did regularly in the boarding.

⟨18⟩

Maharaja Sayajirao Gaikwad of Baroda visited
Satara on 4 April 1933. Bhaurao took his appointment
and invited him to visit the boarding. The car of
Maharaja entered the boarding campus. As he entered,
the flavour of the *Pital* dish infected Maharaja's nostrils.
He suddenly turned to the kitchen while he was walking
across the campus. The flavour of many dishes tempted
Maharaja to make casual inquires about what was being
cooked for the boys.

"Seems delicious dishes being prepared?", he asked.

"Pital is being prepared," somebody informed.

"I'm really tempted to taste it, what did you say?
You mean *Pital* dish." Maharaja expressed his wish.
Bhaurao who was accompanying the Maharaja said,"
Maharaj, you're from Gujarat. Would you be able to eat
the Satari dish? It is very chilly."

"What harm is there if I just taste it?"

Saying so, Maharaja took a piece of bhakari and
tasted Pital and munched a few morsels. Maharaja did
not eat chilly dishes. He became restless and suddenly
started shouting, "Water — water!"

One of the boys immediately served the Maharaja
with a glass of cold water. But the escorting person Mane
Patil inquired if it was filtered water. He said Maharaja

does not drink unfiltered water. All those who were present just kept staring at Maharaja out of surprise. Bhaurao asked one boy to climb the coconut tree and give him sweet fresh coconut water. It helped him to tame down the effect of chilly Pital.

Arrangements were done for the felicitation programme. Maharaja was felicitated in the boarding. Maharaja admired Bhaurao's exceptional work in the field of education and he announced support and assistance to the boarding. He promised to give him financial assistance. He told Bhaurao to meet him after he returned from his foreign tour. As proposed, Bhaurao went to see him but the doctors did not allow him to meet the Maharaja. Unfortunately, he passed away in a short time. It was Maharaja's first and last visit to the boarding. Though Bhaurao did not get financial assistance from Maharaja, he sent his boys to the Baroda Sansthan for higher education. A good number of boys sent by Bhaurao were able to complete their education up to gradation in the Sansthan. The boys were given fee concessions and they got the boarding facilities. Bhaurao started a school in the memory of Maharaja Sayajirao.

Sometimes in between Maharaja's visit to Satara and his demise, Maharaja had invited Bhaurao to visit his Sansthan for a Diamond Jubilee Programme at Baroda. Bapusaheb Nalawade and Mutha accompanied Bhaurao. They were surprised to see Maharaja's glorious palace. A great number of distinguished foreign delegates attended the programme. The escorting man Mane-Patil greeted Bhaurao and his friends at the entrance of the magnificent Mandap. All of them were given grand treatment. Maharaja had little time to spare. But he talked to Bhaurao amicably. He admired his work in the presence of international distinguished guests. It was true that Maharaja had identified Bhaurao's initiating work which was going to change the cultural face of Maharashtra in near future.

19

Gradually people started helping Bhaurao. Those who opposed him in the beginning become his devotees. His father who was unhappy about him, later on became happy. He realized the social significance of his son's work. Bhaurao's wife Laxmibai came from a well-to-do family. But she went through hard times and struggled along with her husband, first for their home and later on for the boarding. Even more than Bhaurao, she paid meticulous attention to every detail of the boarding. She became a real mother of boys and caretaker of the boarding.

Bhaurao resigned his good job at Kirloskar for the sake of education of the poor. Kapur withdrew from his promises. Bhaurao spent everything that he earned during the period. He encountered all sorts of problems. He had no money on several occasions for his personal expenses. He started the boarding at his home in the beginning. Later, the number increased. It was difficult for him to accommodate the boys at his home, so he shifted many of them to a local inn.

Laxmibai played a key role; she was a powerful helping hand to Bhaurao during the difficult times. She did every household work. She washed, cooked, served, nursed boys. Women from Savarn communities humiliated and insulted her because she was serving boys from dalit communities. But she did not take them seriously; she neglected them. She faced insults courageously.

Laxmibai came from an orthodox family. In the beginning, she felt a little awkward. She did everything but with some reservation. She maintained some distance between herself and the dalit boys. But later on

this distance withered away. The boys were now allowed to move freely in the home. Once, she suffered from toothache. It was a severe problem. A Muslim boy Shaikh accompanied her when she went to Pune for the treatment. She took with her food material for cooking but she could not cook because of severe pains. The Muslim boy did everything for her. The boy was excited to see Laxmibai to eat the food he cooked. It was through such situations that Laxmibai came out of her orthodox mentality. She gradually grew and her perspectives became broader and more secular. The boarding boys fondly called her Vahini.

The boarding was shifted to Dhanini's Baug. Bhaurao shifted his family to the Boarding place. Laxmibai guided boys in cooking, cleaning, washing and such household works. Her daughter fondly known as Baby played with the boys. Laxmibai gave up her orthodox attitudes. When Baby was four years old, she played between the home and the hostel. She held a piece of Bhakari from the hostel and took it to the home. She held many such things from the home and ran to the boys and clung to them. The distance between the hostel and the home withered because of Baby's contacts with the hostel. This brought several changes in Vahini's attitudes. She gave up orthodox views. "What's wrong if my daughter played with dalit boys? Why discriminations? All men all equal though they belonged to different castes. If the boys played with Baby in the home, what's wrong in that?" she said.

Once, Vahini's relative was in the home and Bhaurao was out of Satara. She saw the boys and the hostel. While leaving, she asked, "Laxmibai, how many children do you have?" "All these boys are my children", Vahini said pointing her fingers to sixty to seventy boys. The woman wondered at Vahini for some moments out of surprise. What Vahini said was literally true. She loved her boys. When a boy returned from the school, he kept loitering, "Had this boy been in his home, he would have asked his mother for something to eat", she thought so and immediately went inside and brought something to eat for a boy. "Eat this, my son and then run to the school." The boy would be happy as if he had met his mother. She gave eatables to a new boy each time and so every boy thought that Vahini loves him more than other boys.

Principal A. D. Attar was a labour scheme boy. He was allotted some work. He could not complete the work in time. So the boarding superintendent stopped his meals. He warned the boys in charge not to give him food till Anna (Bhaurao) returned the boarding. Attar was a short tempered boy. He got some opium from the town and imprisoned himself in his room. Somebody had told him that he can stop evil thoughts in his mind by taking opium. He took one dose of opium, but it did not work. Then he took the next one. The boys who saw him taking opium doses were frightened. One of them ran to Vahini and told the story. Bhaurao was not in Satara. Vahini immediately went to the place where Attar was staying. She climbed the staircases and saw that the boy was lying on the ground. She took his head on her lap and asked him to open his eyes. But the boy did not respond. She became serious and started weeping. Later, Attar was taken to a doctor and was given proper medical treatment and he was cured. Vahini was pregnant when this happened but she was not scared. She did everything that was necessary. She took care of boys like mother. She saved the life of the boy.

When Bhaurao went out for donations, he did not usually return in a couple of days. He might come back after a week. On such occasions Vahini looked after the financial matters of the boarding. Since all the money spent, the grocer did not give grains on credit. When there was nothing to cook, the boarding secretary asked Vahini, "Vahini, has Anna arrived?"

"Not yet, but he should have arrived by now! What is your difficulty?"

"Vahini there is no grain... we have to feed the children... what to do?"

"Then, what will you do?" Vahini asked in a worried tone.

"Ok? Then you do one thing. Take this golden ornament, get money and buy whatever is required."

Saying so, Vahini gave one of her golden ornaments to the secretary and then the grains and the required food material was bought and the arrangements were done. She had about eight to nine hundred gram golden ornaments but one by one the ornaments were sold. Laxmibai must be the first woman of our country who sold all her golden ornaments for the education of the poor boys. Once again in the absence of Bhaurao the financial position of the boarding collapsed. The hungry boys were waiting for food; Vahini could not stand the situation but what could she do now? There were no any golden ornaments left with her, which she could have given to the secretary. She sat down with her head buried in her laps. After a few minutes, she suddenly got up and took out the Maharashtra, the holy tie of marriage and gave it to the boy, "Take this ornament and make food arrangements for the boys" The boy did sincerely what Vahini told him with a heavy heart. All the boarding boys were shocked. They knew that what Vahini had done for them was just beyond description. Vahini was never able to remake her ornaments. The sacrifice that Vahini showed on such occasions for the boarding boys has no words to describe; it was a sheer boundless sacrifice.

The overload of the boarding work brought greater stress on Vahini. She could never get rest. Her health collapsed. She became weak. She was moreover pregnant.

On one day, she was immediately admitted in the hospital. She was serious and thought that she could not survive. So she called Bhaurao and said, "I don't find any hopes. Let happen anything to me, but tomorrow there is *Padawa* festival. You see that you give boys some sweet."

Later, she operated but it was not successful and on 30 March 1930, Vahini passed away. Mother of boarding boys was no more. Bhaurao lost support of his life. The boys could not control their tears. They somehow reached their place with heavy souls. The boarding became a terrible site for them. It was now a boarding without mother.

⟨20⟩

The number of boys in the boarding began to increase. The expenses also increased with the number. Subsequently, Bhaurao had to wander more to collect funds, so that he could meet the boarding expenses. He had to work hard for collecting funds. He had spent all the money that he had. Moreover, the amount that he obtained from his insurance policies, he spent it on the boys. He began to visit villages and towns. He stayed at residences of his friends to save money. He preferred to eat whatever he could get. He would eat for example *bhaji-bhakari* at a farm side that a farmer might give him.

Once, he was touring in Sangali district. He wandered all day long but he couldn't get a single paisa. He felt depressed but could not give up. He came to the bank of Krishna River. It was getting dark. The night spread and came down on him. He had not eaten all day. He drank bellyful of water and he fell down on the river bank for rest. Next morning, he again wandered for funds. He followed the same schedule for three continuous days but did not give up his work and he was not frustrated either.

Once, he was in Mumbai. He wandered all day and sat down on a bench at a road during night. The midnight passed away. A patrolling police came and woke him up. He asked, "Hey... Who are you? Why are you sleeping on this bench at a road?"

Bhaurao said, "I am Bhau Patil of Satara. I am a teacher. I teach the poor boys of my region."

"Then why have you come here?" asked the police.

"To collect funds for education of the boys; I thought I shouldn't disturb my friends, so I was sleeping on the bench." He said.

"All right... all right. But then don't stay here. This is not a place to sleep."

Bhaurao obeyed the police. He walked away without saying anything. He walked a distance of furlong and slept on another bench. He spent the entire night at road side.

Later, Bhaurao got name and fame among distinguished people. The people invited him. They donated him huge amounts. He submitted the donations to the secretary of the boarding and never used it for his personal or familial expenditure. On the contrary, he used his personal funds for the boarding.

Bhaurao had immense faith in the people. He believed that if you are doing good work and if your work is the need of the society, people come forward and extend their helping hand and you never have any problems in discharging your duty. At the same time, you never get short of funds if your work is significant for the people and if you do your work sincerely. Bhaurao worked with commitment and faith. He always experienced generosity of the people.

Such occasions frequently occurred in the life of the boarding. When there was no foodgrains for the boys, funds came from somewhere or some gave grains or food and somehow things were pulled on and the boarding survived.

Once, as usual, there was no food in the boarding.

Bhaurao was worried because he thought that sixty to seventy boys will have to sleep with hungry bellies. A performance of a play called *Shivsamrat* was fixed in Satara. Shantaram Gupte wrote it and he was from Satara. Bhaurao thought that if the income of one show of the play might be given as donation, it will help him to overcome the existing crisis. Thinking to himself, he reached the Ghate Theatre. The people were busy inside the theater in rehearsals. Bhaurao told them about his Sanstha and boarding. He talked about how he was working in a difficult condition. The owner of the company was impressed by his work. Bhaurao told them that his work was very innovative in the orthodox society. Gupte realized the importance of Bhaurao's work. He donated fifty rupees. It was the collection of one show of the play. Bhaurao gave five rupees as donation to the company from fifty rupees but Gupte returned it to him. Bhaurao remembered the timely assistance of Gupte and Shende all his life.

A similar kind of experience he had in one more incident. R. B. Kale who admired his work extended all sorts of assistance to him. While he was on the death bed, he started a trust of ten thousand rupees and its interest was given to the Sanstha as regular donation. The trust was further expanded by Dhananjayrao Gadgil and R. B. Kale's son-in-law and they added one thousand rupees to it every year.

Later, the Sanstha got donations frequently. Somebody gave land, somebody donated *wadas*; some gave a considerable share of his income. There was a sort of a competing spirit that continued among donors. Even today, Rayat Shikshan Sanstha, which is known for its social work due to Bhaurao's grace and blessings, receives frequent donations. This is a reflection of Bhaurao's recognition and contributions in the field of education.

Humane forces are dormant among people. They are never exhausted. A memorable event must be narrated in this respect. There were about seventy to seventy five boys in the boarding. Two times meals, books and notebooks for each boy, hospital charges... such expenses were huge. This was not a simple matter. It was like running a circus. The eight acre land of Dhanini's Baug was one prime source of income. But that was certainly not sufficient. How hunger of seventy boys could be satisfied for 365 days on a few acres of land? In the beginning, a lot of funds were spent on food and school expenses. There were seventy to eighty hungry growing boys. Their age was growing, so was their hunger. It was indeed difficult for Bhaurao to patch up things and meet the two ends. So, he wandered frequently to collect funds. Some boys got scholarships; some brought something from their homes. But it did not help to bridge gaps in between.

Once, it happened that there was no food, no money. The secretary told Bhaurao about it. It was night. The boys were deep asleep. He was also preparing to sleep. The secretary repeatedly told him about the situation. But he did not pay attention. The name of the secretary was Appalal Shaikh. He did not know what to do. Bhaurao fell asleep soon because of hard work of the previous day. Shaikh at last awoke him. He was irritated, "Appalal, what's wrong with you? Why don't you sleep?"

"Anna, there is no food for tomorrow; how are we going to manage?" Shaikh was worried about tomorrow's breakfast.

Bhaurao spoke in annoying tone, "You had your meals today? Then don't worry about tomorrow. We'll see it tomorrow only. You lie down and go to sleep and don't disturb me." The dawn came, the morning prayers were done. The boys were busy with their mundane work when Bhaurao was walking up and down in the garden.

Suddenly, a loud voice was heard from outside, "Is there Anna inside the boarding?"

"Yes, yes, who are you?", Bhaurao inquired.

"I'm Sadashiv Shete. I'm from Tasgaon. I want to see Anna's Sanstha."

Shete was very happy to see his experiments in the field of education, Self-help co-life, self pride, dignity of labour and such virtues were inculcated among rural boys. This was the novel experiment.

Shete said, "Anna, your work is great. I wish to give you fifty rupees donation for your work." Bhaurao said to Shaikh who was standing beside him, "Appalal, Take the money. You were troubling me yesterday. Arre...man must keep doing good work with faith, and loyalty. Then god is always behind you. Good work never hampers. It often progresses even if there is no money. Take money and run to get food for the boys." Shaikh jumped out of joy and ran out with a smiling face.

⟨21⟩

The boarding was gradually growing at Dhanini's Baug. Bhaurao encountered several difficulties but he did not give up. He continued his efforts. Like a *Rishimuni*, he pursued his work. His experiment was an attempt to reshape the traditional education. His attempt was to relate education to the dignity of labour, to the land, the village, the place from where the boys have come up. He wanted to give lessons of self-help and dignity. He felt that a learner must earn something while seeking education. He must go his own way with his own help, without relying on anyone's support. Poor farmers and labourers usually do not have money for education. So, they are often reluctant to send their children to schools. Bhaurao had visualized that if the bahujan society gets education then poverty, ignorance, superstition will come to an end and the exploitation of the upper classes and Savarna communities will also end. He understood it by his own experiments that education was the best remedy for all social and political ills. His philosophy centred round a few principles like simple living, meaning we must minimize our wants. Secondly, he said that we should not feel shy of any work, meaning any work cannot be either superior or inferior. This was a lesson in the dignity of labour. Next, he wanted his boys to achieve excellence in academic field. He gave importance to character building, sports, social service, love for motherland, sacrifice, brotherhood and such virtues. He dreamt of nurturing such values among his boys. This was his simple educational programme. And he wished to bring it into reality by collective efforts. He also wanted the people to involve into this endeavor.

He knew that poverty alleviates the poor from education and he did not wish it to happen. He believed it precisely that there are talented boys in the bahujan and rural communities. He was firm that education can, if not eradicate, but at least lessen the unwanted impact of evil effects of the caste system that exists in our society. Bhaurao therefore did exceptional experiments. He grouped boys belonging to varied castes, creeds and religion. Dalits, Muslims, Jains, Marathas, Lingayatas, Brahmins and scores of castes came together and lived together. And he was miraculously successful in these attempts.

He wanted his boys to have education that was useful for life. He did not want his students to go for bookish and unreal education. That was how he brought about the novel scheme like Earn and Learn. The boys did a number of jobs through the scheme. They cut stones, took cattle for grazing, sold vegetables in the market, worked under a carpenter or a builder, produced bricks, dug wells etc.

Attempting a variety of jobs through the scheme, he took a lot of care that study of the boys should not be affected. A good number of scholar students participated in the scheme. That was how Bhaurao imprinted on the mind of boys significance of the dignity of labour. He produced awareness and liking for agricultural work. He taught them to use science and technology for development. He persuaded them to use maximum natural resources for agriculture. Thus, he coordinated man, nature and the existing situation through such experiments.

He emphasized principles of simplicity. Besides, he wanted his boys to carry on their studies independently without tuitions. Senior boys taught junior boys. So the boarding boys always came out in flying colours. The result of his boys was always good. They acquired lessons of independence and self-help. Parents and teachers realized that Bhaurao's boys have different faces and identifies. Subsequently, Bhaurao was identified as an important person in the realm of education.

Gandhiji's Satyagrahas was a frequent event in those days. The Satyagraha for Salt had been a terrible blow to the British. The Government had levied taxes on the salt. Gandhiji organized people to fight against injustice.

A similar kind of Satyagraha was organized by Gandhiji. It was called *Jungle Satyagraha*. Participating in the Satyagraha was an opportunity to contribute to the freedom movement. What was the Jungle Satyagraha? The government levied taxes on farmers for grazing their cattle in the meadows. The government auctioned such meadows. The person who took such meadows from the government charged more taxes on the poor farmers. The people therefore decided not to pay the charges levied on the meadows. The Satyagraha was organized at many places. One of the Satyagrahas was organized at Bilashi in Sangli district. The people of the region had prepared to fight for their rights. They had decided to fight even at the cost of their lives. They were ready to do anything to oppose the unjust treatment of the British. They wanted to teach a lesson to the government through the Satyagraha.

The chief action of the Satyagraha was that the agitating farmers will prevent the government auctions. Bhaurao had a call to the Satyagraha from within and so he was desperate.. He had been a true patriot. He always opposed injustice and he had sympathy and affection for the poor formers. Moreover, the Satyagraha was fought in the name of Mahatma Gandhi. Bhaurao had been a devout follower of Mahatma Gandhi. Under his influence, he was wore Khadhi clothes since a long time. He wished strongly to participate in the Satyagraha.

The question of participation became an obsession for him. The only question that disturbed him was the question of boarding. What will happen to the boarding? If arrested, who will take care of the boarding? Who will bring money for his boys? He was confused and was not in a position to take any decision. He could not sleep all night. If he joins the Satyagraha, the boys will be in a terrible time and if he does not, it might imply that he avoids his sense of duty towards the farmers and the nation.

He called some of his boys and said, "Boys, I've

taken a decision."

"What decision, Anna?" The boys called Bhaurao *Anna* with respect.

"Is it about boarding?" One of them asked.

"No, I've decided to participate in the Jangle Satyagraha. The Satyagrahis are meeting at Kameri" Bhaurao said with a cool head.

The boys were frightened. Their faces darkened, they became speechless. One boy, gathering some courage asked Bhaurao, "If you take part in the Satyagraha and if the police arrest you, then ... then, what will happen to us?"

"We'll have to close the boarding then," the other boy said.

"We'll never be able to start a school them. Anna, you please don't go."

"Arre, why are you scared? Your Vahini is there to take care of you", he suggested a way out.

"Anna, if you're away for a couple of days or a week, Vahini can look after the boarding but ..."

"You don't go Anna", boys chorused.

"If I don't go, it will be a great mistake and it will torture me all my life", said Bhaurao reflectively.

He kept quiet for some time. He saw tears in the eyes of his boys. He saw darkness spread in the future of boys.

Controlling his tears, a boy said, "All right Anna. Vahini might look after the boarding but what about the expenses? There is no one who would take care of us. Anna, you please don't go."

Bhaurao's face became very sad and he felt like weeping. Still, he remained silent. He was very much confused. The farmers on the one hand were leading a terrible life. If you don't join their hands, they will be in dire situation. And at the same time, the boys will be fatherless if he goes for the Satyagraha. Being a follower of Gandhi, how could he withdraw!

He called his wife and said, "I 'm going to Kameri to join the Satyagraha."

"When?"

"In a couple of days." Bhaurao said

"And when will you return?"

"I don't know. I cannot say anything. If arrested, I'll return after the release from the prison", Bhaurao said

"Then what are you going to do of this boarding? The boys are from different villages and communities. The people might say that this Bhaurao found a way out to escape from the boarding responsibility. Besides, what about boys?"

Bhaurao said, "Somehow, things will go on."

"Somehow means, how? The boys will give up their education in the middle and you mean, they will go back to their villages? What else will happen?" Vahini was straightforward. She saw clearly the effects of Bhaurao's decision.

But Bhaurao was willful. He did not listen to anyone. He left immediately and straight-a-way reached Kameri where the Satyagrahis were gathering for picketing. The crowd was gradually thickening. The police bandobast was tight. The police and the CIDs were hiding in the civil dresses.

The meeting began. Krishna Patil introduced Bhaurao. Then Bhaurao stood up to deliver the speech. He began to speak; the pitch of his voice was like a mountain.. The people became suddenly attentive. But abruptly the bigger drops started falling down. The sky blackened everything. It grew darker and suddenly it started pouring. The meeting was in a forceful tempo but it came to a standstill due to the heavy rains. People dispersed; the police left. The speaker and chairperson of the programme were on the stage. Bhaurao was obviously not arrested. He came back to Satara. The boys and Vahini were very happy to see him. Their eyes were full of tears. Vahini said that god granted her wish.

After that event, Bhaurao never participated in politics directly. Many leaders and politicians invited him but he never gave up his educational work. He remained away from politics and power.

If the rains did not pour at Kameri? If the Kameri meet was successful? Maharashtra's social and educational picture might have been different from what it is today! We must thank the rains for dissuading Bhaurao from politics.

$\langle 23 \rangle$

$\textbf{B}$haurao's boys were to appear for the matriculation examination. There was no college in Satara. The question was how to provide the boys with facilities of higher education. There was one college at Kolhapur and the others were at Pune. Bhaurao sent some boys to Kolhapur. The lodging arrangements were made in the boarding of Shahu Maharaja. Pune has been a centre of learning and education. But there were no boarding facilities in Pune for his boys. Where could the boys stay and seek education? He decided to start a boarding in

Pune. It must be exactly like the Satara model, he thought. He thought of a boarding in Pune where boys of all castes could live together and follow principles of self–help and co-life, He named it Union Boarding House.

The British Government called upon The Round Table Conference at London when the freedom movement was taking grip. Mahatma Gandhi and Dr. Babasaheb Ambedkar attended the meet. Dr. Ambedkar argued on behalf of the backward, depressed and untouchable community in the Conference. He demanded a right to represent the dalits in The Round Table Conference. He said that Gandhi did not have the right to represent the untouchables. Moreover, he pleaded that the untouchables must be given a separate representation when India gets political freedom. It was because of such a dichotomy, there were differences between Dr. Ambedkar and Gandhi. Mahatma Gandhi started a fast to bring about change in Dr. Ambedkar's perception. Subsequently, unfavourable climate grew in the country. Activists, freedom fighters wanted Gandhi to stop fasting. They took efforts to unify Gandhi and Ambedkar. This became a phenomenal event in the history of our country. To commemorate the event, Bhaurao named the boarding Union Boarding House. The boarding was started for the students who aspired for higher education. The event was very important because Bhaurao expanded his work to a new horizon. It took place in 1932.

The boarding was located at Shivajinager in Pune on the rental basis in the beginning. But there were people in the building who rehearsed dance and music. The boys therefore could not concentrate on their studies due to loud noise. So Bhaurao shifted it at Wadarwadi. Pune Municipality had built temporary sheds at the place. Bhaurao shifted his boarding to this place. There were no toilet facilities. It was at the same time difficult to get drinking water here. But the boys faced odds and found their own ways. The place was adjoined to the campus of Fergusson College. There was one water supply connection near the fence of the college. The boys used it in the beginning. They bathed and even washed their clothes. The Principal of the collage, Mahajani later on provided the boys with a separate water connection. The college spent money on it. Bhaurao used to pay frequent visits to the college and meet the Principal. These meetings gradually developed into friendship. Principal Mahajani invited Bhaurao for lunch and dinner at his residence. His wife donated 151 rupees for the boarding. Bhaurao felt obliged to the couple.

He said, "Mahajani Saheb, you are already helping my boys. You provided them water facility. This was already more than what I expected from you and then why are you giving donation?"

"This is my personal help. It's very small Bhaurao..., please accept it."

Bhaurao's sense of humour clicked. He said, "See Mahajani Saheb, it is we who have been giving *dakshinas* to Brahmins. Today, it is a Brahmin who is giving dakshina to a non- Brahmin like me."

Bhaurao used to wander in the city on bicycle for donations. He would meet merchants, traders, agents, industrialists and told them about his work and boarding and he would ask for donations. Once he got a good response from the farmers who came to sell jaggery in the market.

The boys cooked food by themselves. They washed their clothes. They purchased necessary things from the market. Bhaurao brought several food items such as chili powder, pulses etc. from Satara. The items were prepared by the boys from the Satara boarding.

The distance between the Pune Motor Stand and the boarding was of two miles. Bhaurao generally walked the distance to save money. There was a tonga facility

RAMESH
DESHMANE!

for such local transport in the city. Once it happened, the
bundle that Bhaurao was carrying was very heavy. He had
no confidence to carry it up to the boarding. So he thought
of hiring a tonga. But the tongawalla's charges were
higher. So he walked down the distance without a tonga.

Those were summer days. The scorching heat of the
sun was beyond tolerance. There was a heavy bundle on
the head. It contained a variety of food items like grains,
pulses, different chutneys etc. Usually, Bhaurao walked
the distance from the motor stand to the boarding but
this time it was a different matter. The bundle was too
heavy. There were no shoes either in his feet. So Bhaurao
thought of hiring a tonga. He went near to one
tongawalla who was waiting for a passenger. He asked
him, "Baba, how much you will charge for Wadarwadi?"
Wadarwadi was not a closer place for the tongawalla. He
thought it could be a good deal. So he told Bhaurao the
maximum charges. He looked at Bhaurao and said,

"One and half rupees Baba."

"How much did you say? One and half rupees?"

"Baba, your bundle is heavy and the place is not
nearer."

"No, No! One and half rupees is too much. Make it a little less." And the bargaining went for a couple of minutes.... And finally the tongawalla was ready for a deal of one rupee and twenty five paise.

But Bhaurao was not ready, he said. "I'll give you one rupee only."

"I've to feed my horse Baba, besides I too have my own belly" Said tongawalla.

"That's true, but my pocket is also not full of money. I can give you one rupee only, see if it is possible."

The tongawalla was reluctant and Bhaurao was also not ready to give twenty five paise more. Bhaurao at last took the bundle on his head and said, "Let it be Baba. I don't want tonga at all. I'll buy something for my boys with one rupee and twenty five paise. My legs are strong enough and I'll reach the place in time." Saying so, Bhaurao started walking.

There is one more interesting anecdote of this kind. Once, Bhaurao was as usual carrying a heavy bundle containing a variety of food items. It was surprising that Bhaurao hired a tonga this time. The horse pulling the tonga was old. At a slightly ascending place, the horse found it difficult to pull the tonga. The tongawalla began to whip the horse ruthlessly. Bhaurao pitied the horse and could not tolerate the tongawalla's torturing.

He said, "Yeh...Tongawalla, stop your tonga here only"

"Why Dada.... Don't worry .. the horse is adamant"

"No.. No. You please stop... and you first stop whipping the horse, the animal can't complain, can't speak.. Why are you whipping it? Don't worry, I'll pay you all your money, but stop whipping the innocent horse."

"But,... but ... Dada ....."

Bhaurao paid the bill, lifted the bundle on his shoulder and walked towards the boarding.

24

Education is a tool of social change. Everyone must get education for which he or she does not have to pay. Bhaurao thought that to get quality education, the teachers must get appropriate training in teaching skills. So he organized Teachers' Conference at Angapur in Satara district in 1921. He presided over the conference. Three resolutions were passed in this conference.[1] Every village must have a school.[2] Teachers from bahujan communities should be appointed to teach rural children and 3. Every teacher must receive training in teaching skills.

Bhaurao declared in the conference that for providing training to teacher from bahujan communities, he would soon start a training college at Satara. A teacher from a village should not just teach but he should also play a role of a guide to the villagers. Bhaurao's announcements came into reality in 1935.

The British Government was celebrating the silver jubilee programme on account of the successful completion of King George's rule in India. The Collector of Satar, Hamid Ali was planning to organize a programme at Satara. Ali had respect for Bhaurao's works in education. He visited Bhaurao's boarding several times. He admired his boys because they were free from addictions. He liked them because they were simple enough and did their works by themselves. He asked Bhaurao if he was interested in celebrating the silver jubilee programme of King George.

Bhaurao said, "If you are going to give *silver*, I'll definitely celebrate the programme." He further said, "We don't get trained teachers in rural regions, so it is necessary to start a training college for teachers."

Ali accepted Bhaurao's proposal and gave a green signal to start a training college. He gave donation for the college. The programme was organized in Dhanini's Baug. A training college was thus started at Satara. It was named after Mahatma Phule. Training colleges in rural regions like Kusur and Mahuli were also started. A school for the training college also came into existence. It was named after the second president of the Sanstha R. B. Kale.

Rayat Shikshan Sanstha was registered while the training colleges came into force. The Sanstha put in black and white its aims and objectives. Satara's Collector, Hamid Ali became the first President of the Sanstha. Bunyan tree became its emblem. An executive body consisting of twelve persons was formed. The government hesitated in the beginning to provide grants to the college. So the executive body of the Sanstha shouldered the entire expenses in the beginning. The Principal K. S. Dixit was Bhaurao's opponent but Bhaurao won the hearts of teachers. Principal Dixit later became Bhaurao's devotee all his life. Several of them worked without salaries. Principal Dixit suddenly passed away in 1953 and Bhaurao became the chief patron of the Dixit family. He met relatives of the Dixits and said, "I knew Babasaheb (Principal K.S. Dixit) very well. I knew his commitments to the Sanstha. He has done great service to the Sanstha. I'll give you twenty rupees per month on behalf of the Sanstha." And Bhaurao sent twenty rupees per month to Mrs. Dixit unfailingly. The training college was the first example of its own kind. It went on without government grants. It worked successfully with the support of the people.

Bhaurao admitted Brahmin boys also in the college. He provided them all necessary help. The poor boys from the Brahmin communities came to Bhaurao. Once, a Brahmin teacher took admission in the college. It was the Second World War period. Prices of all commodities were rising. Inflation in the market was beyond control. Grains were not available in the market. Even if you find somewhere, it was smuggled and their prices were unaffordable for a common man. The government distributed grains at rationing shops. But it was of low quality. The Brahmin teacher was staying at Satara during his training period with his wife and two kids. His one kid was always sick. The teacher therefore did not attend the classes regularly. The Principal fined him. Bhaurao came to know the details. He went to see the teacher. He visited his home. Bhaurao made arrangements. He sent a sack of Jawar and rice to his home. He said, "Now, you can pay more attention to your study, attend your classes regularly, take care of your kids. Don't feel awkward to talk about your problems. When you have difficulties, come and see me but don't give up your studies, don't think negatively." Bhaurao's encouraging words strengthened mind of the teacher. Tears appeared in his eyes. These were tears of gratitude towards Bhaurao. The teacher completed his training successfully and achieved remarkable grade in the examination.

The year 1942 emerged and Bhaurao felt strongly to start a teachers' training centre for women also. If a woman is educated, the entire family is educated. Bhaurao knew the truth. Education enables women to learn to manage her familial matters more effectively.

However due to rising financial pressures and the increasing number of students and branches of the Sanstha, Bhaurao had to wander constantly for more donations. The pressures made him helpless. Though he wished strongly to do something for girls and women. But he could not do so as planned and deliver concrete results.

Once, Begun Sharifaben, wife of the Collector Hamid Ali and the first President of the Sanstha were conversing. Bhaurao opened the topic.

"Bhaurao, you are a very selfish person. You only work for educating males. What about women?"

"What do you mean?"

"Bhaurao, have you done anything for women?", she asked a straightforward question.

"Yes, you are right. I haven't."

"Have you done anything for girl students? Let go the questions of women from our society."

"Yes, that's true. We haven't done much for women too."

Bhaurao was a open mined man. He accepted his limitations wholeheartedly. Begun Sharifaben said, "Bhaurao, I'll not talk to you till you do something substantial for women. Bhaurao, you look at me as your younger sister. So you have to do something for your sister."

Bhaurao took it as a challenge. And he kept his words he gave to his sister-like person Sharifaben. He started Jijamata Adhyapak Mahavidyalaya, a training college for girls. The college opened a space for rural girls of the region and they began to receive training in education. He also started a separate hostel for girls so that the girl students can stay at Satara and complete their education. Lessons of self-help and self-reliance were also given to the hostel girls. Besides, Bhaurao played wonders by bringing remand home and girls from criminal families in the hostel. He brought about miraculous changes and transformations among such girls. Such girls improved and also achieved remarkable success in their personal and family life. The people gradually changed their attitudes towards such girls.

Bhaurao held the view that the primary education is the foundation. So, the primary teachers play an important role in inculcating values among learners. He therefore tried to empower primary teachers. He fought with the government on many occasions to increase salaries of primary teachers and to provide them with more facilities. He organized several conferences to pursue such issues. Through such programmes he expressed a sense of gratitude and solidarity towards them. The primary teachers in turn helped Bhaurao to start boarding at Dudhagaon and Herle. They sent bright and smart students to him. They played an important role in producing social awareness among villagers. Bhaurao himself had been a teacher. He toured extensively. He met ministers along with veteran teacher activists like Acharya Donde. The primary teachers were getting fifteen rupees as the monthly salary in those days. Bhaurao took tremendous efforts and there was a hike of 12 rupees in the salaries of the teachers. He then organized a conference at Dhule in 1945. He became a patient of blood pressure since then. When he arrived at Pune Railway Station, he felt sick and was prepared to sleep on the platform itself. Then he was bed ridden for two months.

Bhaurao thus did everything that was possible for primary teachers. His training colleges in rural region were a blessing to the teachers.

<25>

Bhaurao was a simple-minded and straightforward person by nature. Paradoxically, he was a stubborn and short tempered man. If his wrath explodes, it was difficult to control him. At the same time, he was kindhearted and a man of sympathetic sensibility. Especially, for the boarding boys, his love knew no bounds. He was like a true further to them. For disciplining them, at times, he was very strict and hard-minded. The boys knew well the real nature of their guru.

There are numerous incidents when Bhaurao came

up with several things for the boys. Once in the Dhanini's Baug, a poisonous snake stung a boy. With plenty of patience, Bhaurao took him to the doctor immediately and he was treated properly. He was terribly disturbed. "Doctor, what'll happen now? My boy must be saved at any cost." He said desperately.

The doctor said, "Bhaurao, don't be panic, there is nothing to be worried. I've given him injection. Take care; don't allow him to sleep. He must be awake all night." Bhaurao nodded his head and took the boy to the Baug. He kept a close watch on him all night. He used to lie down under the bunyan tree in the Baug. He did not give food to the boy. Another boy was stung by a snake the next morning after the prayers. Again the same things! No sleep all night but Bhaurao did not complain. He was fresh and energetic the next morning because he loved his children more than himself.

There are a number of such instances. Once, the result of the matriculation exam was declared. There were four boys who stood in the first ranks. Bhaurao was very happy. His joys knew no bounds. It was the result of Bhaurao's efforts. When everyone was celebrating happy moments, an unpleasant incident took place. A boy called Bhoite fell down in the deep well of the Baug. It was a hundred feet deep well. Bhoite was lifted from the well in a cradle. He was injured seriously. He was bleeding profusely. Bhaurao, a huge mountain like strong man wept like a child when he saw the condition of his boy. He never wept in his life even when he attempted to kill himself in Kolhapur. But when he saw Bhoite, he could not control his tears. The boys gathered around him and they could not know what to do. Disasters and cruelty of fate turned Bhaurao into a feeble person. He could not save the boy. Bhoite passed away. Boys did a huge funeral procession. Bhaurao was totally lost. He could not recover from the tragedy for a long time. He was never able to remove the slur from his mind that he could not save Bhoite. His love for the boys was beyond anyone's imagination.

Bhaurao found good things in his children. He did everything that was possible for them. He was literally obsessed by them. He always felt bad because he thought that he was not in a position to give them nutritious food. He was both father and mother to them. It was a sort of his instinctive sensibility. At times, if he found some money with him, he spent for his boys.

Once, when he was in Kolhapur, the boarding boys came to meet him. Bhaurao made inquiries about their studies, health and needs. Bhaurao knew it that his boys lived in difficult situations and faced many odds. He knew it that they could not afford to live like the other college boys. He saw that one boy was not seeming good. He asked him what was wrong with him. He advised to see the doctor immediately. Then, he said, "Come, let's go out for a walk."

The boys asked, "For a walk means where?"

"We'll go to a hotel and eat your favorite dishes", said Bhaurao.

Saying so, he took all of them to a good hotel. He served them their favourite dishes which they had longed for. This was a shock to the boys. He told his boys that they were studying in a college and like their other friends they could at least pay a visit to a hotel. While he was talking, his eyes were wet.

Bhaurao's love for his boys knew no discriminations. He loved clever and bright students as much as weaker students. With patience, he asked his weak students to appear for the exams till they passed. Like a father he brought sweets and gifts to them. He brought books for them. One boy in the Kolhapur hostel was weak in his studies. His performance in the exam was not up to the mark. He failed in Enter–Exam. Bhaurao did not get angry but encouraged him to reappear. He again failed. Bhaurao was not disturbed because he had seen him studying sincerely. But he failed in a few subjects. He sent him to another college.

He wrote to him. "You don't get disturbed because you failed. I don't feel that there is something wrong with you. I saw that you took all possible efforts. But you don't give up and don't get disheartened. Don't think that I'll be angry. You appear again and do your studies properly." The boy appeared for the third time and got through. This was a moment of bliss for Bhaurao. What Bhaurao did, must not have been done even by the boy's real father. It is just incomprehensible and unimaginable tolerance and compassion!

He had also a few favourite students. Barrister P. G. Patil was one of them. He was studying in the seventh class in 1937. His school was nearer to Bhaurao's residence. One day, during the middle recesses, Patil went to see Bhaurao. It was raining outside. The climate was chilly.

He saw P.G. Patil and said, "Arre..., it is so cold and you haven't put on any extra clothes that protect you from cold. And why have you come to me?"

"Just to see you."

"Do you have a sweater?"

But at once Bhaurao thought to himself that how a village lad could afford to buy a sweater! He got up and took P. G. Patil with him and came to Maniyar's shop.

He said, "This boy is very bright and clever. It is cold these days. Give me a good sweater for him." He bought a good sweater for P. G. Patil and said, "Now run to your school or you might miss your class." Of course, Bhaurao could not afford to buy sweaters for his all boys who were equally dear to his heart.

An annual gathering programme was celebrated in Chhatrapati Shivaji College. The gathering programme is an opportunity for the college boys to put on good clothes and do a lot of fun. It was like a marriage ceremony for girl students. Girls would do all *shringar* in such a programme. The boarding labour scheme boys did not have good clothes to put on and compete with the city boys.

On one such occasion, Bhaurao called the boarding boys and bought good new clothes suitable for each one of them.

He asked them, "My boys, when do you celebrate your college gathering programme?"

"In about eight to ten days Anna", one boy said.

"Then, are you taking part in the programmes?"

"Yes Anna! Many of us are taking part in items like singing *powada* (a ballad), *bharud* (a folk song) etc."

"My lads, where do you have good clothes for such programme?", Bhaurao asked.

"Yes Anna, we have our clothes," somebody said pointing to the clothes put on their bodies.

"The same clothes we wash a day earlier for the programme and ..."

"Is that so!" Bhaurao said getting up. "Come, let's buy new clothes for everyone this time." Saying so, he went out and bought new good clothes for every boy. This was a great shock to all boys. Tears appeared in their eyes. Boys therefore addressed Bhaurao as *Teerthroop*, meaning *true father*.

Like true father, he conducted marriage ceremonies of his boarding boys. Though his health was not good, he went to Mumbai to attend Dr. B. S. Patil's marriage ceremony. He told others that he was attending his son's marriage. Similarly, he conducted marriage ceremonies of M. J. Nikam and P. G. Patil. Marutrao Raut went for intercaste marriage and Bhaurao's participation in this ceremony was remarkable. He encouraged intercaste and inter religious marriages. P. G. Patil's marriage was conducted at Char-Bhinti in Satara. Bhaurao was then sick and he was in Kolhapur. But he was insistent to attend the ceremony. "I look at this boy as my son, so I want to attend the marriage in any condition." And he attended the ceremony! He was an enthusiastic person in the ceremony. He took interest in a number of things and shouldered several responsibilities. He usually took voluntary interest in such ceremonies. He visited homes of newly married couples to bless them. He gave them some tips of advice. As fatherly figure of the Sanstha, he had innumerable children and their happy lives gave him pleasure. The delight that he sought from such visits was just beyond description. Bhaurao was broadminded. His love for boys was a great source of energy to him. He never expected anything from them. He was the richest man because many boys loved him more than their real fathers. Hundreds and thousands of boys worshipped him as god. Great are those boys who got his comradeship!

Bhaurao began his work with a boarding in 1924 with one student. Later, this number increased to seven and gradually it went up to seventy to eighty. This was not as much extensive work as compared to the number of villages. One district approximately consisted of about one thousand villages and Bhaurao's work was spread in four districts. So Bhaurao thought that bringing one or two boys from a village to Satara and giving him education will never enable him to change the picture of the society. What about hundreds and thousands of children? What about those who are good and well to seek education but could not attend the school? If you want to improve bahujan communities, you have to educate the entire society. You cannot bring all of them to Satara. How to bring the children from thousands of villages together and teach them? A better way out would be to take the school to them instead of bringing them to the school. You have to instill awareness among the parents and the citizens from villages at large about education. You must produce favourable climate for education. It will affect villagers at large and there will be an initiation of thinking. Then villagers might send their children to the school. You could minimize superstitions and ignorance of illiterate community through education.

Bhaurao thought that this was the proper composition of his programme of education.

The first Congress Ministry came to power in Bombay State in 1937-38. Annasaheb Latthe was the Finance Minister. He was Bhaurao's rector-teacher in his Kolhapur days. Bhaurao met him and said, "We must do something sensible for children of bahujan communities. It must be a dynamic programme." Latthe said, "Bhaurao, you bring a plan and we'll surely do something."

Bhaurao met Vitthalrao Ghate immediately. He was the Deputy Director of Education Department. Mr. Ghate respected Bhaurao and he knew his works. Both of them produced a plan. The plan was known as *Voluntary Primary School*. It implied that wherever the government does not have a school, a school will be opened there. A qualified teacher will be appointed, some funds for schools will be given by the government but its administration work will be done by a private institution. Bhaurao decided to start schools in several interior parts of Satara district. Many young boys had completed their education up to seventh standard but they were unemployed. Bhaurao appointed them as teachers. Hundreds of such young boys got jobs as primary teachers. Almost all of them were from rural regions.

In the interior parts of Maharashtra, all villagers were illiterate. When they received letters, they were unable to read them. They had to travel longer distances and attempt several tasks like cut bigger logs of wood into smaller pieces for fuel and such others. After doing such hard tasks, the literates were pleased and then they read their letters. Bhaurao knew it well. The pathetic situation exploited the poor and illiterates. So, he was very much decisive to end the situation by taking education to interior parts of rural regions. It was a challenge to him and he accepted it.

People said, "Bhaurao it is a hilly area."

He said, "Will do."

"There is no road to the village."

"We will find ours", he said.

"There are wild animals like lions and tigers."

"Let there be!"

"There are diseases spread in the region,"

"No problem."

"Medicines are not available."

"Will do!" This was his policy.

Sometimes, villagers themselves opposed to the idea of starting a school at their place. They were worried that if their children went to school who would look after the cattle, collect fodder and fuel etc. They were worried that who would provide a place for a school and spend money on books, clothes, teacher's food and residence etc. But Bhaurao got cooperation from them.

The villagers being illiterate, they asked their gods for a favourable or unfavourable response whether to start a school or not in their villages. A flower was placed on god's statue and if it fell on right side of the statue, it meant a favourable response and if it fell on the left side, it meant an unfavourable response. It was a sort of religious custom. Bhaurao used the folk practice to get a convincing response from god to start a school. His basic intention was to educate rural folk.

Once, Bhaurao visited an interior region of village in Patan tehsil with a young teacher. He wanted to start a school in the village. The village was thickly surrounded by hills. Thick forests, trees, rivers, fountains and wild animals surrounded the village. It was alienated from other villages and human habitations. He called a meeting of the villagers and convinced them how important it was for them to start a school in the village.

A villager asked a question, "Why do we need a school? We don't need it?"

"Government takes money as education tax from you, at least for that reason you must ask for a school in your village. Your children will become literate, educated and wiser."

"Then who'll work in the farm?" somebody asked. "Who'll take care of the cattle if the children go to schools?"

Bhaurao sorted out such difficulties but new difficulties rose up. The villagers said, "That's true what you say, but there is no place for your school in our village."

Then Bhaurao said, "We'll start the school in a temple or a hut."

"Then where your teacher will live? That's again a problem!"

"It's not a problem; he'll also live in a temple."

"And what about his daily bread? Who'll feed him? Who'll take care of him?"

The villagers looked at teacher and school as something they were doing a favour to Bhaurao.

"See, my friends, the teacher will cook himself, stay in the temple. He'll live where there would be his school; or each one can cook one day for him. Tell me if your guest visits you, don't you give him food and shelter? So the teacher can take food at one home each day and he can live in a temple."

These words of Bhaurao convinced villagers and they became ready for the school. Teachers walked down longer distances. They carried necessary food items with them. For example, they carried sugar, salt, oil, floor, grains, Jawar and rice with them. There were no proper roads. They walked untrodden tracks full of thrones and several barriers. In some villages, villagers provided teachers with meals. In course of time villagers were happy, when they saw their children were able to read and write. As a result, they began to respect teachers.

Later, the same teacher became their friend, philosopher and guide. They did not do anything without their advice. They took every advice from the teachers like calendar, holy day for a particular work, their private family matters etc. They asked him everything. The teacher became a central person for them. He removed ignorance, prevented them from numerous superstitions, evil customs etc. He persuaded them importance of education. He never took disadvantages of villagers. Bhaurao declared a new scheme. It was known as *there would be a school where there would be a temple.*

Villagers helped Bhaurao and his teachers. They provided him with a place to live, food to eat. They were happy to see their children reading and writing. Number of schools started by Bhaurao increased up to 578 in 1950. Around more than 1200 teachers worked in such schools. Bhaurao sent salaries to the teachers through money-orders. He admired their work. The government too recognized the great work that Bhaurao was rendering.

Bhaurao paid regular visits to his schools. He started a department in the Sanstha. It was known as the administration department. He travelled in bullock carts or used horses to visit his schools as there was no other transport facility available.

Once, Bhaurao was visiting a school located at Anawale village. There was no means of transport available to him. It was not possible to travel by a bullock cart either. At last, he decided to travel by a horse. He had no money but a horse was hired for five rupees. The horse was weak. Bhaurao sat on the horse. Shantaram Kakde, his student escorted him. The horse could not walk the road. It was a local road in a hilly area. Bhaurao was a huge man and the horse could not carry him and he fell down. The boy instead of giving support to Bhaurao, burst our in laughter. Bhaurao became angry,

"My boy, you are laughing instead of giving me a helping hand?" Of course, the boy helped him and again Bhaurao sat on the horse. They somehow reached the village. Darkness fell soon and they stayed at a village on road.

Bhaurao selected good teachers and provided them training. After the training, he helped them to get government jobs. During the post-1947 era, education was made free and compulsory by the government. Naturally these schools were included in the government block. The work of the Sanstha expanded. Bhaurao thus took education to each hut and cottage located in rural regions of Maharashtra.

⟨**27**⟩

    Bhaurao's work began to acquire social and cultural recognition. Attitudes of people changed towards his works. He offered dignity to labour. He demanded that every student must work and earn his own living. It became the central principle in his philosophy of education. Eight acre of land that he owned for the boys to work appeared now small enough. He was unable to provide with work to every boy. So he thought of more land for his boys. The land near *Char Bhinti* (Four walled) belonged to the government. The district collector Hamid Ali was Bhaurao's friend. He was in Satara. There was a possibility of his transfer. Bhaurao had not asked anything from him. So Ali decided to talk to him.

"Bhaurao, you haven't asked anything for the Sanstha. I wish to give you some land. There are two options, one is a place called Hajerimal Open Land and the other one is the government place called Char Bhinti. You are free to make the choice."

Bhaurao said that he would like to go for Char Bhinti Everyone was confused. "What are you saying Bhaurao? The place is nothing but a huge black rock and what are you going to do with this black rock? Are you going to break it?"

"Yes!" said Bhaurao. "Yes, I want to break the rock." The collector without any debate gave the huge black rock to Bhaurao. Bhaurao was very happy. He got the rock-place and started the second branch of Shahu Boarding. While breaking the rock, Bhaurao told his boys that he was not breaking the stone but centuries old practices of enslavement, walls of religions, castes, evil customs and traditions. What he was breaking was not just rock! He planted coconut trees. Banana garden bloomed here and vegetable greenery spread all around. The boarding boys worked in the garden in the morning and broke rocks in the evening. The campus is marvellous today where beautiful statue of Karmveer stands signalling his message in the background of a huge rocky hill and a row of magnificent buildings add to the splendour to the campus.

One rich farmer sent his son to the boarding. When he visited the boarding, he saw his son was breaking stones. He became disheartened. He requested Bhaurao that he would pay more fees but his son should not be given such work. To which Bhaurao replied, "Look, you need not pay me extra fees but your son has to work with other boys. Self-help is a part of education. A farmer's son must never deter from work. Man's true beauty lies in his work, his body writhing in sweat. It is his true *Alankar*."

Bhaurao was reacting spontaneously. He was speaking with a pinch in his belly. The farmer said that his son had never done any work. He did not even take a glass of water for himself. Knowing this, Bhaurao became very angry and he burst out. "You see, it is true that every parent wants his child should not be given any physical tasks but if a parent is to be served his child with a glass of water, it is a great defeat of education. This cannot be called education but poison. We must throw this poison out. At least, I take care that such poison should not affect my children. I wish to produce young men who would be healthy by mind and spirit. I don't wish that children should be so weak and fragile by mind." Bhaurao's outburst left a deep mark on the farmer's mind. His eyes sparkled with some light. There was a total change in his attitudes and perception towards education; He realized the significance of labour in education and its prime role in the formation of children's personalities. While leaving, he thanked Bhaurao for opening his eyes. He said that he would never complain to him. He told him that he understood importance of dignity of labour.

There is one more interesting incident. It was the time when Bhaurao had already started the first college of the Sanstha, namely Chhatrapati Shivaji College in Satara. To avail of water on the campus, he was digging a well. There appeared a black rock of huge size in the ditch of the well. Everyone was busy in breaking it. There were five *Wadars* who were breaking stones. Those were summer days. The scorching sunlight was burning skin and brains of boys. The boys were working ceaselessly for eight hours a day. Some of them dug and some carried containers of mud. Physically well-built boys helped

Wadars to break the stone. Explosives were used to break stones. After the explosions, Bhaurao looked into the well to observe how much portion of the stone was broken into pieces. He stood at the edge of the well and gave directions to each one. He would say, "Arree ... those who have water in mind and body will definitely discover water in belly of the mother earth. You must have a strong will and then the work becomes simple enough. You are hard working boys. I'm very happy to see you working in scorching sunlight. I'm proud of you. You are true sons of the soil." While giving voice to his inner spontaneity, he took part in the tasks and helped boys.

While the project was in progress, a veteran educationist visited the campus. When he saw boys working he said, "Bhaurao, if you give boys such hard physical work, they will not pay attention to their studies. Subsequently, they will fail to achieve intellectual excellence. Such physical tasks are harmful to their intellect."

Bhaurao did not agree. The boarding boys were attempting all sorts of work. They laboured day and night and did all odd tasks from cutting wooden logs to digging a well. Then where did their intellectual development hamper! On the other hand, their brains became hard and were ready for progress.

Bhaurao thought for a moment and then said, "I don't want elite boys who shun away from physical work. I don't want this kind of education. Such education produces feeble and weak-minds. I give education in exchange of their work. If people get something without any work, it does not weigh any importance. My simple philosophy is the philosophy of self-help. I want boys to work sincerely. My education-programme is the programme of self-help and self-reliance. This is a new experiment. I respect boys whose palms are hardened by physical work. Knowledge that you get through bookish channels is devoid of life. It is artificial and false. But knowledge that you earn through your own blood of labour is true. It takes you to your dignity and pride till the last breath of your life. These are my attitudes and perceptions."

Yes, it is true that Bhaurao never agreed to the idea that physical labour hampers intellectual capabilities of individuals. He used to give ancient references of how students stayed in ashrams and did all sorts of physical work and obtained education. Was that education of secondary status? He believed that physical exercise makes your brain vibrant and fresh. It helps you to develop your spiritual and psychological capabilities.

The education that one gets through one's labour offers a sense of dignity and pride whereas the education that one gets through begging makes one weak and feeble. Anything that you get free does not enable you to take it seriously. That was how Bhaurao laid down his philosophy of self-help. He was in search of honest boys who followed the principle of self-help. He felt that he would provide such boys with food for two times and necessary material for their education as an exchange towards their work. He believed that the boys who did physical work, their minds and spirits would become harder. He conceived of an ideal citizen as a person who worked honestly for his family, village, his fellowmen, society and his motherland. He felt that knowledge that you obtain from experience of life is greater than that of books.

Bhaurao did whatever he said. His ideas were very clear. He believed it with a pinch in his belly. So the listeners were charmed by his speeches and talks. Today, the government, the universities and educationists plan to bring about changes in the existing educational system. They are giving more priorities to the vocational aspects of education. Bhaurao did it long ago. It shows that how Bhaurao had a prophetic vision of education.

28

Several institutions and the government recognized Bhaurao's works. His Sanstha was engaged in producing ideal citizens and was serving the nation. The government also took cognizance of his works. His attempt of inculcating values and virtues like self-help, co-operation, patriotism, equality and humanism was recognized. The first Chief Minister of Mumbai State, Balasaheb Kher appreciated his works. The CM respected him. He paid frequent visits to the Sanstha, made inquiries about his health. He thought that Bhaurao's work was unique and characteristic. The government gave the Sanstha special yearly grants. It was known as Efficiency Grants. It was 1200 rupees yearly. It must be noted that this was the only boarding in Maharashtra getting such grants from the government.

Morarjibhai Desai had acquaintance with Bhaurao. He was then the Revenue Minister. When he was on tour in 1938, he stayed at Dhanini's Baug instead of the government rest house. He admired Bhaurao's educational work. He also agreed that Bhaurao was imparting education of higher quality.

Ten acres of land near Char Bhinti was donated to Anna. He was happy to note that the society was recognizing his work. So he thought he must start his own high school. There were two schools in the town. It was at this time, Sayajirao Gaikwad passed away. Anna started his first school in his name. Maharshi Vitthal Ramaji Shinde and Dr. Dhananjayrao Gadgil attended the inaugural programme.

On this occasion, Dr. Gadgil said, "Satara is the centre of Western Maharashtra. When a few people progress, the nation does not develop. It is only when masses march forward and leadership from masses emerge, then only society can go forward." For Sant Gadage Maharaja's *Pravachan* mammoth crowd gathered. People from neighboring villages attended his Pravachan. He spoke on Bhaurao and said that Bhaurao worked all his life for the poor. He gave a third eye of knowledge to them. His work was greater than his own work. He pointed out that when the children of farmers sought education, they progressed rapidly. You spend lot money on religious Yatras. You should spend it on education of your children. It will be the great *Punyakama* to the Sanstha. This country will reach its peak of progress only when activists like Bhaurao will be produced.

The Sanstha started new branches such as Maratha School and training colleges. These branches were like true laboratories where the Sanstha activists got enough training in the field. One more exceptional experiment Bhaurao did at this juncture of time. He decided to admit children who were in various government prisons. He was of the opinion that children in prisons become more criminal-minded. The company of criminals empowers them and they become worse. The prison officers dissuaded Bhaurao from such ventures. They told him that his efforts would be futile. On the contrary, such boys would affect good children of the boarding. But Bhaurao did not give up. He had trust and confidence in himself. He told the officers exactly the opposite. He said that there are all possibilities that the criminal children might be changed in the company of his boarding boys.

He told the officer, "You give me your children. I'll look after them in the boarding."

"Bhaurao, your attitudes are good; I understand that. But these children are not normal like yours."

"All are not bad", said Bhaurao.

"Some of them are orphans and some are mischievous. So instead of improving and reforming them, it is wrong to keep them in the prison. I'm sure I'll definitely improve them in my boarding. I've come to meet you with this intension in my mind."

"That's all right Bhaurao, but these boys are criminals. They are vicious, ill-tempered and worst. If you treat them kindly and with love, they'll deceive you and run away from the boarding. They'll pollute good climate of your boarding and in turn your boys will be infected by them."

"I don't think so. I wish to do an experiment." Bhaurao did not turn away from his decision.

The officer finally said, "See Bhaurao, you give a thought to it once again cool headedly before you take any decision. We'll give you all expenses that the government spends on each boy."

"See officer, if the boys are treated with love and affection and if good boys accompany them, I feel confident that they will improve."

The officer had no other option than to allow Bhaurao to take the boys with him. He brought them to his boarding. The boys surprisingly under Bhaurao's care and affection achieved tremendous progress. They were transformed miraculously.

Bhaurao did succeed in what he said. His strong convictions were behind his work. He not only provided boarding and educational facilities but he patiently helped them to complete their education. Some boys from this lot became college teachers and some captured high-profile jobs in government sector. Bhaurao's immense faith showed to the government that it is always possible to kindle a torch of humanism. It might be a little dim due to unfavourable conditions but it could never be extinguished

    Bhaurao opened more boarding, more primary schools, more training colleges, more secondary schools. Primary education was taken to doors of the poor. More number of schools increased workload of the Sanstha. Government grants were not enough and so the financial pressures increased. Bhaurao went for more donations. He thought of farmer as a broadminded donor. His work was recognized in rural regions. There were plenty of donors who voluntarily donated. These people became members of the Sanstha. There are a number of memories and anecdotes in this respect. A few of them are given here.

Vitthalrao Deshmukh from Mahuli Sangli district invited Bhaurao for marriage ceremony of his brother Dattajirao Deshmukh. During the ceremony he submitted the entire dowry amount of eight thousand rupees to the Sanstha as donation.

On this occasion, he told the people that Bhaurao is the modern Dnyaneshwar who attended the marriage ceremony of his family. He said that it was a rare event for him. Bhaurao gave education to the poorest of the poor and so he was giving the entire dowry for the noble work of education.

Saying so, he gave eight thousand rupees to Bhaurao. The people clapped wholeheartedly and gave a voluntary sanction. After a couple of weeks, Bhaurao met Vitthalrao again for money. He said, "I'm in deep troubles," Vitthalrao unhesitatingly gave Bhaurao one thousand rupees. He had just collected the amount selling a few sacks of agriculture-produce. This was his trifling support. He donated seventy eight acre of land to the Sanstha. Bhaurao got frequent assistance for boarding school and training college from Vitthalrao. Such was Bhaurao's image in his own times. Mahuli, Vitthalrao's village was turned into an educational centre by Bhaurao.

This is the story of a donor who had donated voluntarily. But there were several people who were reluctant to donate. They admired and flattered Bhaurao but did not have any wish to help. This might be perhaps because of their bitter experiences. Probably, the money that was donated was not properly used and so they turned bitter. The experiences of Jayajirao Shinde of

Gwalior's Maharaj were of similar kind. Maharaja had three palaces and about one thousand three hundred acres of land at Shrigonda and Jamgaon in Ahemadnagar district in Maharashtra. He had sent a few boys abroad for higher education but he had bitter experiences. The boys did not show loyalty to the Maharaja after they returned with foreign degrees. With such an unfavorable background, Bhaurao paid a visit to Maharaja when he was on the tour to Pune. Though reluctant, Bhaurao persuaded the Maharaja that his donation to the Sanstha

would be of greater value. His palaces would be turned into graveyards soon if they were not used properly. The wooden pillars would be stolen as fuel, whereas the Sanstha would use it for educational purposes. The Maharaja was convinced by Bhaurao's words. Though reluctant in the beginning, he donated the Sanstha three Wadas and a land of one thousand three hundred acres with his own expenses.

The Maharaja was impressed by Bhaurao's sincere and heartfelt words. He realized it from within. He understood that Bhaurao is indeed a hard-working man and he really had concerns for the bhaujan communities.

Bhaurao had been an expert in extracting donations from those who did not donate easily. He did not give up his efforts. He had a sort of an art in getting into consciousness of donors. He spoke and presented things in such a way that the donor did not say *no* to Bhaurao. Mr. Kapur of Kirloskarwadi was a budding industrialist. Bhaurao helped to start his industry. He had promised him that he would donate some amount from his income regularly. But he did not keep his promise. Later Bhaurao got donations from Mr. Kapur also.

The Mayor of Pune city, Bhaurao Sanas helped the Sanstha frequently. He collected funds in his own capacity. He also spared a lot time for the Sanstha. He served Bhaurao during his illness and took care of him on several occasions in Pune when he was hospitalized. Bhaurao stayed at his bungalow for several times.

Baburao Sanas' brother Bapusaheb was the rich man. But he had not donated a single paisa to the Sanstha. Bhaurao met him and he did not talk to him directly. On the contrary, he talked about how his friends and relatives had donated and extended help in different forms. He also mentioned names of a few who were poor enough. They also helped the Sanstha. This indeed humiliated Bapusaheb. Bhaurao was a good presenter. He used his entire capacities to convince donors. Bapusaheb was already convinced of Bhaurao's works. His presentations however affected him and he got emotional towards his words. He donated ten acre of fertile land to Bhaurao. Besides, he donated a separate open land to start a school.

When Baburao Sanas learnt it, he was shocked, "How did you do this Anna?", he asked. "It was one of the wonders of the world that a person like Bapusaheb turns into a donor." Bhaurao just smiled and didn't say anything. Bapusaheb remained a lifelong activist of the

Sanstha and he built up a huge school building in memory of his father.

The example of Bapusaheb Sanas as a donor was one extreme end, whereas Dadasaheb Patil of Karjat, Ahemadnagar district and Mukadam Tatya's example were at the other end. Both of them had already donated. Mukadam Tatya used to get tremendous money but a lot from it was wasted on addictions and the rest was spent on religious works.

Sant Gadgebaba advised Dadasaheb to give some donation to the Sanstha. One high school, one training college and two boardings were started due to Tatya's efforts at Kusur. Mukadam Tatya gave Sanstha one Vitthal Mandir and twenty five acres of land. Because of such donations, the Sanstha started many branches at Karjat.

Bhaurao was like a saint. He gave up all familial responsibilities. He devoted his entire life for the Sanstha. He collected donations from generous donors and masses of the region and spent them on the Sanstha. He spent money at times for students who were abroad for their higher studies. If salaries of a branch are not paid, Bhaurao paid them from the donations. He never went for loans and so his works never came to a standstill. Whenever a crisis arose, he rushed for donations. He wandered every door from the rich to the poor, the farmers to the workers. People gave him whatever they had because they were sure that their money was used for education of the poor.

One could visualize that how difficult it would have been to send ten boys abroad for higher education in such times of crisis. Bhaurao did it sincerely. It was a miracle of the generosity of the existing society.

Once, a crisis erupted. Bhaurao needed money badly. All his work came to a standstill because of paucity of funds. The jaggery-merchants of Kolhapur came forward

and gave him a fund of twenty five thousand rupees as an award to his social and educational works.

Once, Bhaurao had been to Baramati. He had called a meeting of the activists. Bhaurao was a huge man, the way he led his ideal life was like that of a Rishimuni. His clothes were simple He spoke in mountain–like voice and his work was so great that people were impressed by his magnanimous personality. His speeches charmed them. In a meeting at Baramati, people were moved by his works. People voluntarily donated him to pursue his works. One rich person in the meeting gave Bhaurao one hundred rupees. Bhaurao marked that it was a small amount from a rich person. So he did not say anything on his miserly attitude. He said, "Keep it, keep it with you, I'll take your donation not now but sometimes in future." The rich man was happy. He thought that he saved his hundred rupees. He immediately put the amount in his pocket. But Bhaurao did not ask the man for donation deliberately. He met people whenever he visited Baramati but he did not turn his feet to the rich man's doors. The man got hurt and understood his mistake. While he was bed-ridden and there was no hope of his survival, he called his son and said, "I wanted to donate some amount to Bhaurao of Satara. That is my last wish. Before I die, you please go to Satara and donate five thousand rupees to him." The son respected his father and did what his dying father said. This example shows that there was tremendous power in Bhaurao's personality. His negation also had a profound impact on the people.

There was a handsome building in Satara. It belonged to Malojirao of Phaltan. Several *Sansthaniks* and the rich people had such mansions and Wadas at Satara. The Phaltan Maharaja's building was known as Phaltan Niwas. Bhaurao went to Phaltan and met the Maharaj. He requested him humbly to donate the building to the Sanstha. The Maharaja did not respond positively. Later he just kept the issue hanging. He said *yes* on several occasions but did not do anything.

Bhaurao was annoyed. At last he spoke in a high pitch sound and in a straightforward manner. He thought to himself that what would happen. The Maharaj won't give the building. The effect was opposite. Malojiraje was very happy. He said, "I see that people keep flattering for their selfish ends and such people usually surround me. I seldom find people who pinpoint my mistakes and limitations. A person who does not have any selfish motive can only speak in this fearless tone. Bhaurao, I'm very happy, I am donating you the Phaltan Niwas Building and a ten acre of land to your Sanstha. Besides, I'm also donating a fund of five thousand rupees for repairs of the building." Malojiraje kept his words. This was the place where the first high school and Chhatrapati Shivaji College was opened. A number of plans and programmes for the development of the Sanstha were worked out at this place. This was the impact of Bhaurao's fearless temperament. He never went to any one for donations helplessly. On the contrary, his huge and magnanimous personality attracted hundreds and thousands of people to donate to the Sanstha. In one of the election campaigns, though Bhaurao criticized Malojirao publicity, he was felicitated by his Darbar. Bhaurao held the view that donations should not bring pressures of obligations or the donor should not have a feeling that he is a sort of authority on you. Bhaurao was a fearless man. He acquired the trait through his work and from the Gandhi-thought. He was not frightened to talk truth in presence of a huge donor in bitter or insulting remarks, let he be any person.

Once, Bhaurao had to go to Kolhapur to attend the birthday programme of Chhatrapati Shahaji Maharaj. There was a huge crowd gathered in the palace to greet the Maharaja on the occasion of his birthday celebration. Everyone wanted to garland him. They bowed down to express respect towards him. Bhaurao did the same but while bowing down, he smelt that the Maharaja was drunk. He suddenly reacted, "Today at least you should not have drunk Maharaj." The Maharaj just smiled but those who stood beside him broke out against Bhaurao. But Maharaja said, "Let him speak, he is like my Aba (father). I look at him as my father." The Maharaja knew that Bhaurao was a close associate of Chhatrapati Rajarshi Shahu Maharaj. The same Shahaji Maharaj donated one hundred and thirty acres of land and lacks of rupees to Bhaurao.

Rayat Shikshan Sanstha was absolutely born and developed out of donations. The government also provided megre grants but it was largely administered on the donations. Some gave cash, some donated land, some buildings and some one day salary. Many devoted workers of the Sanstha spent their entire life without taking salaries from the Sanstha. Activists like Bapusaheb Nalawade, Rambhau Nalawade, Ismail Mulla devoted services to the Sanstha. Bhaurao's unique method was that he was able to draw donations from the most miserly person to the poorest of the poor and he accepted anything happily for welfare of the Sanstha.

There are hundreds of such memorable donors and it was due to their well wishes the Sanstha made rapid progress. Even today the Sanstha accepts such donations. There are illiterate people where generations and generations have never seen the faces of the schools, still these people donated their megre contributions to the Sanstha. This shows broadmindedness of the people and the greatness of Bhaurao's work. Such wholehearted social support does not emerge so easily, for which virtues such as sacrifice, service, character, updatedness, good sense and good nature are required. Bhaurao possessed these virtues on which the Sanstha was built up.

$\langle 30 \rangle$

The bunyan tree of Bhaurao's educational work was expanding consistently. He started primary schools in innumerable villages. Then he opened secondary schools at some places and adjoined the primary schools to them. Boarding's were also started. To inculcate virtues among students like self-help and dignity of labour, he provided boys with farm work in each unit which became partial earning resources for the Sanstha. In order to provide training to teachers, he opened training colleges. Now, Bhaurao thought of opening a senior college.

There were two important reasons that forced him to start a senior college. The first reason was that the first batch of Sayajirao Secondary School of 1947 was going to face the matriculation examination and the same batch had the problem of college education. During the period, there were very few colleges and the students were sent to such colleges only on one's own expenses. Sending students to colleges located at Pune, Kolhapur or Baroda was an expensive matter for Bhaurao. It was difficult to send all students to colleges either to Pune or Kolhapur and this was not the question of one year now. It would recur again and again. Besides, the age group of the students was such that they might be attracted to many temptations. For Bhaurao, it was also a question of good company that his students might get. The boarding students were different. They behaved in a very different way than others. However, there was every possibility that they might go astray. The adolescent age is a stormy age. Children are triggered to innumerable temptations and keeping such children away from his eyes was not good according to him. That is what he thought. It is an age when boys do wrong things. One wrong step and the entire life can turn topsy-turvy. The children who had been brought properly in the school may not follow the right path necessarily in the college campus. So Bhaurao did not want to run a risk. He thought that all such problems could be overcome if he could start his own college at Satara. Then he need not send his boys to any other place away from his eyes. His eyes would be always set on them. Bhaurao therefore announced that he was going to start a college when his pocket was empty as usual. He made such an announcement in 1946. The announcement obviously shocked everyone.

His friends wondered at his announcement. They told him that starting a college was not just difficult but it was impossible. They advised him not to go for such an adventure. One of Bhaurao's close friends said, "Anna, what announcement you have made? How is it possible to start a college?"

Bhaurao said, "That's why, the announcement is made. When you say something publicly, naturally the responsibility falls on you to complete the work that you promise. This is how we keep working. We did several things till now which appeared impossible to us in the past."

"We will require huge funds".

"Funds will come", he said.

Dr. Dhananjayrao Gadgil also convinced Bhaurao not to start a college. He said, "Bhaurao, you don't go for college. It is like looking after a white elephant. That's not possible for you."

Then Bhaurao's efforts for the college doubled. He applied for opening a college through proper channel. The application was sent to Mumbai University. In course of time, the University sent the commission. The chairperson of the commission was Prof. G. R. Paranjape. He was the chief of Royal Vidyan Sanstha of Mumbai. The other member of the commission was Wrangler D. C. Pawate who had worked as the Vice Chancellor of Karnataka University.

Bhaurao faced such stalwart personalities, the members of the University Commission. And it was unbelievable that the members themselves instead of making observations and putting forward suggestions, Wrangler Dr. C. D. Pawate, the Chairman of the commission said, "Anna, we are so called educationists, trifling and bookish people. We understand *the printed education*. But you have been a real educationist. You have studied a treatise of real life. We are so small and trivial before you that we need to take lessons of education from you." Obviously, the members gave a favourable report. He named the college after Chhatrapati Shivaji Maharaj, the historical hero of Maharashtra. The college was started in the place called the Phaltan Niwas building. All the necessary repairing work of the building was done.

The financial problem was a major one. Bhaurao started a state-wide tour for the financial assistance. He said that his college was going to provide free education. It would be a residential college. The students will work and they will get education through their own earnings. He told people that for such a new kind of college, he wanted financial help. The people gave him unprecedented response. Hundreds and thousands of people donated Bhaurao to start the college.

Knowing that Bhaurao Patil of Satara wants to start a college and he is in need of huge funds, one rich person of a neighbouring place invited Bhaurao and said, "See Anna, if you are going to name the college I suggest, I'll give you entire funds necessary for the college." To which Bhaurao gave a very audacious reply. "I'll not change my decision. I live on certain principles. I keep words and follow promises. It's true I may be in difficulties but I'll give the name to the college, which is already finalized. I'll change my name but I'll not change the great name given to my college, Chhatrapati Shivaji Maharaj's name!" The rich man was stunned by Bhaurao's words. His arrogance built on wealth and money collapsed. He began to respect Bhaurao and later he became his follower.

Bhaurao visited several villages and towns. He delivered speeches, talked to people and convinced them to help him. He would say:

"Our children must learn."

"Higher education is very important. More higher education; better the chances for our children to progress."

"Can we send our children to Pune and Mumbai for higher education?"

"Are the expenses of higher education at Pune and Mumbai affordable to us?"

"There is not a single college for our village boys here."

"My college will be free from other expenses. You don't have to spend money on your children's higher education. Every student will have to work in my college. They will be given education in exchange of their labour."

"The parents don't need to sell or mortgage their land for the sake of their children."

"I want donation from you, however small for this strange and different college of mine."

Bhaurao got unexpected response. Hundreds and thousands of donors came forward and extended a hand of co-operation to him. Dhondoji Patil of Nagzari village from Satara invited him. He was the first donor for the college project. He gave Bhaurao five thousand rupees and said, "Anna, you start your college. Our children must learn. I'll give you more money if you need." And Bhaurao was able to complete the construction of the first building of the college.

In the beginning, there were only seventeen boys but later on the number in the Arts Faculty was more than 1500 to 1600. The college was adjoined with a hostel and Bhaurao made it compulsory for students to stay in the hostel. He made it equally compulsory that every student must attempt physical work. It was through his work his bills of lodging and boarding was paid. It was through such novel schemes, Bhaurao completed big projects like huge buildings of the college, hostel, a swimming tank for the boys, a big well for drinking water facility, flattening of land for agriculture purpose etc. Bhaurao personally supervised the work. The boys grew vegetables in the farm and they sold in the market. The boarding vegetables had good market value. This was an exceptional experiment in the field of education across the country. But there was weak response to Bhaurao's programme. As a result, he faced a financial loss, loss of lacks of rupees. In course time, he made boarding an optional category. The government provided fee concessions to the poor boys. It helped him to a great extent. The number of students in the college obviously increased. The District President of the Local Board provided a new place for the college and some funds.

In the beginning, the college began in Phaltan Niwas building. There was no separate building. The construction work was yet to be started. As Bhaurao was walking along the road with slow pace, he saw Balasaheb

Desai. Bhaurao said, "I was thinking of you only and was planning something; and the same thing happened. Come let's go by a tonga. I've an important work."

"But, Anna, what are you going to do at night?" It was eight o 'clock.

"You first come along with me, then I let you know." Saying so, the tonga was brought to the college campus. There was complete darkness; a few boys of the hostel were asked to bring the lanterns.

In the bleak light of the lanterns Bhaurao said, "Balasaheb, break the coconut. Today, we have started a good work. Today, we have started the construction work of the building for Chhatrapati Shivaji College."

Balasaheb followed Bhaurao's order. After the short programme, somebody said, "Anna, you did not see any *Muhurt.*" The tongawalla who was standing beside said, "Today is *Amavastya*"

"Amavastya and *Punav* are same for us. When a pure thought comes in your mind, that day becomes Punav for us."

Balasaheb said, "Anna, it's good, I broke the coconut but if the construction work of the building is not completed, my image will be marred."

Bhaurao said with confidence, "Balasaheb, when Bhaurao Patil brings something in his mind, he never gives it up. Why cannot we complete this work? Is this a government construction work?"

And Bhaurao did succeed in what he said. The work was completed within ten weeks. The new building of the college came up and the place got a splendorous look. Krantisinh Nana Patil and Jagganthrao Bhosale who were in Satara inaugurated the new college building. After 1958, the faculty of science was started in the college. Dr. V. S. Patil who gave up his job from Dharwar joined Bhaurao's Sanstha; so that the science college could be developed. Dr. C. D. Deshmukh was the

President of University Grants Commission (UGC) who visited Satara. Dr. Deshmukh himself had been Bhaurao's devotee who provided special grants and another huge building was constructed which was inaugurated by Dr. Rajendra Prasad, the President of India. Bhaurao showed through such ventures that if you have a strong will, you can succeed in any task which might appear impossible.

There were about only fifteen high schools in Satara district around 1940. Out of which five schools were located in Panchgani town. The schools were for the rich and elite classes. The rich sent their children to such schools. The rest of the schools were in town places like Satara, Karad, Phaltan and Wai. Hence, a boy from an interior region had several difficulties in getting even the secondary education. It was not possible for him to leave his home and go to a town place for education. So Bhaurao started Maharaja Sayajirao Vidyalaya at Satara. However, it had its own limitations. He thought to start schools in various villages of the district so that the children of various villages might join such schools. Bhaurao produced a network of secondary schools in the district. Wherever it was possible, he started a school.

For example, he would visit a village and tell villagers that he was going to start a school. The villagers obviously were happy and extended him all help. It was his policy that the students must labour for the school. When it was not possible for him to give work to students he said, "Give me a barren land I'll turn it into a green one." People responded to his call and a boarding was produced out of it.

Self-help, co-life, self-cooking and simplicity were

his principles. A high school at Lonand was an excellent example of this kind. There was not a school in ten miles campus of the town. A generous donor called Ghodke donated the land for the school. The government also provided funds. The merchants of the town incurred education tax on sales and purchases of different commodities. The Maharaja of Phaltan provided substantial support. The teachers of the school collected donations through performances of drama programme staged by Rayat Natya Mandali at various places of the region.

Mukadam Tatya of Kusur took part in the project and extended help like land, money etc. to start a school at Kusur. The Kusur School became an ideal centre of the Sanstha. The education officer of the region admired efforts of the people. He said 'The Kusur School is a dazzling example in the map of India.'

The school at Devapur was a similar example. This is a drought prone village of Maan tehsil in Satara district. There was a large lake called Rajewadi Lake. The government auctions for tilling lands were declared at the lake campus. The rich farmers took the lands in higher rates and as a result, the poor farmers had to work as land labourers in their farms.

Bhaurao started a school for the children of the poor in the region. He got some land from the government. He also started a boarding for the students. Tribes called Sanagar were in good number in the region. The Dhangar and Ramoshi people were reluctant to send their children to the school. The orphans and the children who were pushed into evil and bad business were admitted in this school. He started the mission with his usual lessons of self-help. Orphans and criminal children played wonders. Bhaurao had therefore a soft corner for this school. Farmers of the region had established societies and were able to till the land. The government provided help to the farmers. Tata Trust came to help of the farmers. Dr. Dhanajay Gadgil played a key role in this context. The trust helped the farmers to till the land and provide training for agro-based business and cottage industry.

Bhaurao looked at the school as an ideal example of the Sanstha. He therefore took guests, educationists to this school. Once, the Vice Chancellor of Gujarat University visited the school and he was wonderstruck by the great mission of Bhaurao in the field of education. He said that he felt like a small child before the towering personality of Bhaurao.

He further said, "We get abundant funds. We construct huge buildings and we teach our students by charging plenty of fees. But Bhaurao visits such places where no one would dare to go. His places are strange and these are the real places where the poor live. Where there are no facilities, not even basic things like drinking water; people are illiterate, backward and ignorant and Bhaurao overcame them and he succeeded in producing a *nanadanvan* in such unfavourable situations. We are very small people before him. His work is towering and excelling in comparison with what we did"

Mr. and Mrs. Gadgil, the couple was a significant participant of Devapur project. They visited the place whenever they found time. On many occasions, the couple stayed at the place and mixed among illiterate farmers. They held the view that the Devapur project was an image of the belief that any constructive work, if you work hard with missionary zeal, was possible on this earth. The Devapur was an illustration of an unprecedented experimentation; it offered charm and magic to the simple and naive people of the soil.

A similar example was followed at Ashta in Walwa tehsil in 1944. Bhaurao started a school in Ashta and there was no dearth of donations. People came up with building material; some gave bricks, some ceiling covers, some dug a well for water supply, some worked for a school building. Dnyandev Kadam donated his land for the school. Students worked in construction work of the building. A head-master was sent for the school; his name was Joshi. The people belonging to Jain-creed were in good number in the village. "Give us a Jain head-master, then we'll give donations," said the people. Joshi said, "That's all right". He went to Bhaurao and said, "Anna, transfer me to any other school because people demand a Jain-head-master. The school will prosper and get good donations if you give a Jain-head master." Bhaurao lost his temper and said, "What nonsense you are talking about? If you're selling your principles then say that Bhaurao Patil is no more. I don't need money. Those who work with me, they should not think of caste, religion, creed and such things. Joshibhau, you're mine, you belong to me, you go there and construct building. I'll give you money and be fearless. The Sanstha is behind you." Bhaurao kept his word. He sent 40 thousand rupees within three months and Joshi completed the building work.

There was a huge hill spread around the bank of Malharpeth River. There were several *Wadi-Vastis* located around the hill. People called the hill Dambarkhadichi Tekadi (meaning a hill that looks as black as tar and is composed of black huge rocks). The people thought that the hill is full of ghosts and a gathering of the ghosts is held in the temple at the hill. Bhaurao wanted to put an end to this superstition. He wanted to produce fearlessness among people. He decided to open a school on the hill itself. Lalasheb Patankar of the region helped him. He appreciated Bhaurao's plan. Thakkar Bappa, a follower of Mahatma Gandhi came to inaugurate the primary school. The villages of the neighbourhood provided help and donations. The villagers collected about more than 3300 rupees. Thakkar said on this occasion that if our country produces more true social workers like Bhaurao, it will undergo unheard transformation within a short time. He reported what Gandhi said about Bhaurao. Gandhi held the view that Bhaurao Patil's work was fundamental and revolitionary. He was a true social worker.

Thakkar Bappa visited Malharpeth with Bhaurao on 3 June 1945. A huge procession of bullock-carts was taken out; a chariot was called for the procession. The school was renamed Thakkar Bappa Primary School for which Bappa himself donated one thousand rupees. What is surprising to note here is that when the school was inaugurated, the school building was not constructed yet. But within twelve hours duration of the night, a big shed of 58 by 14 was completed by the edge of dawn. Sag-wood, about fifteen thousand pieces of ceiling items, stone, cement etc. was shifted to the huge hill. People like Dnyandev More, Keshwarao Kadam, Govindrao Sutar, Balaku Desai, Sidoji Patil, and Patankar undertook tremendous efforts in the mission and a temple of learning came up within a night where people thought ghosts lived. Bhaurao named the hill Gandhi Tekadi. This example was a great inspiring force to the people who worked in the field of education. It also showed that how villagers' efforts, if motivated properly, could lead to a work of social cause. This branch was a symbol of an attempt where participation of villagers for a social cause was remarkable.

At Pravaranagar in Ahmednagar district, the first Sugar Factory of its own kind in our country was started. It was a farmers' factory. The owners of the factory were the farmers. It was an ideal project. This was the contribution of Vikhe Patil and Dr. Dhananjayrao Gadgil. They were the inspiring forces behind the project. They were also the central parts of the project. The mushrooming of sugar factories in Maharashtra began after the success of the Pravaranagar Project.

Bhaurao attended a meeting of farmers in the campus of factory. He said that the factory will enhance life standard of farmers. They will be benefitted financially. But at the same time, he warned them that if their children do not get good education, they will go astray. Bad habits and addictions will kill them. He therefore declared that he was going to open a high school in the campus. He expected that behind each ton of sugarcane farmers send to the factory, they should pay four *annas* as education tax. The farmers granted Bhaurao 's demand. The school was opened. Following the ideal, high schools at Shrirampur, Kopargaon, Ashoknagar, Rahata and Kolapewadi were also opened.

Workers of Kirloskarwadi wanted Bhaurao to start a school at their place. People came forward and collected huge amounts of donations including the land. They collected ten thousand rupees. And accordingly, a school was started at Kirloskarwadi. In the similar way a school at Shirwal was also started. Thus began a marathon of opening schools at different interior places. Subsequently, with support of people, the Sanstha opened schools at Solapur, Khanapur, Rukadi, Pusegaon, Karjat, Apshinge, Aaitawade, Dahiwadi, Manchar, Tadsar, Walhe, Baramati, Hadpsar, Shrirampur, Poladpur, Sakharpa, Malakapur, Waphgaon, Wade, Bavi, Vinchur, Palshet, Juchandra, Pare, Marwade, Bhui-Bawada, and Mokhada.

Bhaurao stressed three important things while he opened schools. He started schools where there was extreme need of the region. Secondly, he opened schools in tribal regions for the tribal communities like Koli, Kunabi, Dhanagar etc. Thirdly, he appointed teachers who had sought training from his own schools and colleges. According to him, his students who became teachers knew tribal and rural life well. Besides, they were industrious and held high ideals. He therefore considered them as better teachers.

He made tribal and rural folk to participate in his mission. He provided them employment and meaningful assignments. At times, he did not hesitate to ask them to raise funds for the Sanstha. It is interesting to note that he unhesitatingly attended marriage ceremonies in the areas where he worked and collected donations for the Sanstha. He accepted small donations from the salt workers in Mumbai. If somebody gave him bullock cart for transportation, Bhaurao took it as donation. What is striking to note here is that Bhaurao imprinted on the minds of people that they must give something of their own for his mission. He thus broadened his canvass of participation. He collected funds but his forms of donations were determined by regional situations. As a result, awareness of education grew among farmers. Landless labourers and tribal thought that this was not Bhaurao's individual work. So, all of them participated in his work wholeheartedly. The awareness boosted idea in the minds of people that it was through such efforts that missionary work of the Sanstha will be carried on. Thus, Bhaurao succeeded in instilling social awareness among people of his times.

The Sanstha opened 329 High Schools, 76 Boardings and 7 Training Colleges. A small tree developed into a huge tree with its myriad branches. It is a rare example of its own kind; an educational complex with so wider network. There is no such parallel example across the continent and perhaps even in the world.

⟨32⟩

Mahatma Gandhi was assassinated on 30 January 1948 by Nathuram Godase, a Brahmin youth. The news spread across the country like a whirlwind. Masses went berserk and were uncontrollable. Masses from bahujan communities instigated madness and irrationality. Violence triggered against the Brahmin community. They set their houses on fire and looted them. The violence spread in Satara district. Bhaurao contacted the district collector Ramanand Swami Bharati and organized a Shanti Yatra to shun people away from untoward incidents.

Balasaheb Kher, the C M delivered a public speech on 8 February 1948 in Pune at Shaniwarwada. It was a emotionally charged speech in melodramatic style. He said, "How one could dare to say that Brahmin community will be uprooted and doomed completely if the murderer of Gandhi was a person from that community. I'll not allow anyone to attack the Brahmin community till the last drop of blood in my body. I'll take all efforts to protect the community." The CM spoke in emotional bewilderment.

The news flash of the C M encouraged Bhaurao to continue his work to establish peace in the bahujan communities in Satara. On 12 February, a huge public meeting was gathered at Gandhi Maidan to pay homage to their leader. The district collector Swami Ramanand Bharati attended it. Bhaurao spoke on the occasion and told people to maintain law and order and social peace. But he attacked the views of the C M.

He said, "The murderer was a Brahmin, so it is absolutely wrong to attack the community. It is against the ideology of Gandhiji. But I must tell the CM that he alone cannot do it. The common people can only protect the Brahmins. He must understand that he does not represent only the Brahmins. If he says so, it shows his casteial approach." He thus expressed his disapproval towards the casteial language used by the CM. He ironically asked, "How much does Mr. Kher possess blood in his body; say about a few liters, or more than that. So, how many Brahmins will be protected by his blood? The CM should not use such casteial language. I am a follower of Gandhi for more than forty years and I am following his principles. I myself, my activists and innumerable students are taking efforts to protect the Brahmin community."

The newspapers flashed Bhaurao's speech with different colours. There were some conspiring groups against him. They sent prejudiced texts of his speech to the government. These people were jealous of Bhaurao's mammoth like works. Some of them from the town took disadvantage of his speech and tried to mar image of the Sanstha.

The government immediately stopped the grants of the Sanstha. The Home Minister Morarjibhai Desai toured Satara district and reported the government that the situation in the district was anarchic. He spoke in Satara at Gandhi Maidan. A huge crowd gathered. People were curious about what the minister was going to talk about Bhaurao. Morarjibhai talked for a long time. He spoke fifteen minutes on Bhaurao and his

Sanstha. He poured his anger on him.

Bhaurao did not withdraw. He toured the district and told people about how deliberately the things were distorted. The government stopped grants of the Sanstha and consequently financial situation of the Sanstha became crucial. The boys found it difficult to get their daily bread. The tension grew everywhere. But the Sanstha people including teachers supported Bhaurao. They said that they will work even without salary. They felt that the Sanstha should not suffer.

Bhaurao toured across the State for funds when the government stopped grants. The government brought ban on Bhaurao 's public speeches. Then he followed a different device. He would visit a place and people would gather around him. Then he told people that he was hungry and he wanted some money to buy a day's meal. If they don't have any money, they can give him some grains. He told them that he was teaching their children and they were starving. He had no funds and no grains to feed them. He asked them if they were going to allow them to die of hunger. Bhaurao 's appeal changed peoples' attitudes. He collected huge sacks of grains and fifty three thousand rupees. The Sanstha worked smoothly without the government funds. Donations came to the Sanstha regularly.

The Maharashtra Congress Committee passed a resolution at this juncture. It stated that the government has done injustice to Rayat Shikshan Sanstha by stopping its grants. As a result, there has been a great blow to the educational cause of the bahujan communities. The committee expressed protest against the decision of the government. The leaders like Shankarrao More, Keshavrao Jedhe, Tulshidas Jadhav, V. D. Ghare told the government that it was injustice to the Sanstha, which was educating the bahujan communities of Maharashtra. The left front leaders helped Bhaurao. At this critical juncture of time, Balasaheb Desai, the President of Satara Local Board started grants of five thousand rupees every year. Dr. Dhananjayrao Gadgil and Bhausaheb Nalawade provided precious guidance to Bhaurao during the period. In the meantime, leaders like Bhai Madhavrao Bagal, Shankarrao Dev, Swami Ramanand Bharati, Jedhe, More took efforts to bridge up the gap between the government and the Sanstha. But it did not work. On the contrary, reverse developments took place. Annasaheb Latthe took part in this work but nothing came out of it.

Neta, a daily from Sangli favoured Bhaurao's side and wrote an editorial firing the government's wrong education policy. The editor of the daily was B. L. Parab and Balasaheb Bhosale. The criticism of the editorial worked well. But the government banned daily. At last, several MLAs came together and decided to put an end to the issue. The CM got the report about the developments. Consequently, he immediately started the grants to the Sanstha. When a question was raised in the Assembly about the same, the CM reported that he has not stopped the grants. He told the press that an order has already been issued to sort out the problem. The decision of the CM was welcomed with a thumping majority in the Assembly. Yashwantrao Chavan also played a key role in this question.

Gandhi had written a letter to Bhaurao 21 days before his assassination in which he had admired his missionary work in the field of education. Bhaurao was trying his best to bring in Mahatma's ideas into reality through his work. But the Sanstha suffered because of such developments. The government sent a letter and started the grants of the Sanstha from 30 January 1948. It was the day on which Gandhiji was assassinated. It showed that if you have unflinching support of the people, you could go forward with a torch of success. Men achieve greatness facing disasters and such moments prove their testing times.

Dr. Dhananjayrao Gadgil said in one meeting that whenever the Rajsatta (political power) goes berserk; it is people like Rushimunies (Anna) who control it.

Jayprakash Narayan visited the Sanstha. He admired Bhaurao 's works. He said that Bhaurao 's works showed the practical reflections of socialist theories. His students and his experimentations taught him several things. He said, "There are no casteial walls, no fees, instead the students get education through their own earnings, life of simplicity; these principles ought to be the basis of Indian educational system. Bhaurao Patil showed a super highway of education to the nation through quaint journey of his life."

There was a unique feature in the methodology of Karmveer Bhaurao Patil. He always started his work from the foundation. He developed that foundation when the requirements rose up. He never had any sort of exhibitionist attitudes. He never made a show of his work. He had understood that farmer and bahujan communities of Maharashtra were illiterate and no progress was possible if the communities remained uneducated, illiterate and backward. He therefore decided to take education to the doors of the bahujan communities. To do this Bhaurao first started boarding; so that children can come to the place and live there and get education. For availability of good teachers, he opened training colleges. Then he turned to the primary schools. He opened primary schools in innumerable villages. Where could the children go for higher education after the matriculation education? So, he opened colleges for them.

It is significant to note here that Bhaurao did not start a college in the beginning of his career as Lokmanya Tilak did it. He started a boarding, then primary schools, secondary schools and then he went for training colleges, so that his teachers would get training in teaching skills. Finally, he went for regular colleges. Thus, he started his mission of education right from the bottom.

He opened Azad B.Ed. College at Satara about 45 years ago when colleges of Satara and Kolhapur region were affiliated to University of Pune. The university commission paid a visit to the Sanstha and the permission was granted to start the college.

Bhaurao had no enough funds to pay the deposit in the university for the college. It was a question of twenty five thousand rupees. It was a huge amount in those days. Bhaurao and Rambhau Nalawade brooded over the idea all night about how funds could be raised. Bhaurao was against going for a loan. The night darkened and there was no flash of light. They did not know what to do. They kept asking each other about how to sort out the problem. Who would give such a huge amount? How to make a proposal? "Can we go for a loan?" asked Rambhau.

Bhaurao said, "You know that I'm against loan".

"Not loan Anna, but let's borrow from someone", said Rambhau.

"It is the same, my lad, whether you call it *Pithal* or *Zunaka*. Both mean the same thing", said Bhaurao.

Night grew dark. But there was no solution, no decision. The difficulty remained unsolved and the dawn broke. Finally Bhaurao said, "See Rambhau, who is that Bank Manager? You ask him about the loan."

The next morning, both met the manager. They told him about Sanstha's financial situation. The manager said, "No problem, your Sanstha is so great that I'm ready to give you one lakh rupees on my own risk. I'll give you loan. Send the documents, I'll sanction it." Bhaurao was happy; he got up and the straight-a-way went home. Rambhau did the follow up work and went back to Bhaurao at 4 pm. He was in his deep sleep. That was how the BT College came into existence.

A similar kind of event took place when five thousand rupees were to be deposited for the same college. A gentleman from Mumbai, a massage doctor came to see Bhaurao with a cheque of five thousand rupees. He narrated an incident that how one student met him and the doctor came to know about Bhaurao's work through him.

Bhaurao as usual was in Shivaji College. The boys were working in a neighbouring farm side. A new posh car came and stopped where Bhaurao was sitting in company of the boys. A middle aged gentleman got down from his car with folded hands. He said, "I'm coming from Mumbai. I'm a doctor by profession. I'm a massage-doctor. I am specialized in this field of treatment. I have numerous patients who pay me good amounts for their treatment. The rich man, Sir Purushottam Thakardas of Mumbai is my patient. He paid me five thousand rupees recently as fees towards his treatment. One of your students met me in Mumbai when your memories came to my mind. I immediately took the decision. I took my car out and came to see you Anna. I want to give you the cheque of five thousand rupees." He handed over the cheque to Bhaurao while he was speaking to him. Meanwhile the boys working in the farm gathered around Bhaurao.

Bhaurao said, "I was unnecessarily worried; god understood my difficulties and sent you to me. What's your name Sir?"

"I am Dr. R .K. Bhosale. I have my hospital in Mumbai." The doctor introduced himself.

Bhaurao said, "I don't know how to thank you.

Later Bhosale donated the Sanstha two times and each time he gave fire thousand rupees. Bhaurao felicitated Dr. Bhosale in Satara in the presence of Dr. C. D. Deshmukh. On this occasion, he said while addressing his students, "if you work selflessly for social transformation, people themselves come to you for all sort of help". The students were greatly influenced by what was happening. The B. Ed. College was named in memory of Maulana Azad who had extended co-operation to the Sanstha on behalf of the Central Government.

Bhaurao faced a similar kind of situation when he started another college at Karad. The college was named after the great Maharashtrian modern saint Sant Gadage Maharaj. Bhaurao was then not a well known person. He had not achieved much recognition in his work. Since then Gadage Baba paid frequent visits to Bhaurao's Sanstha. He delivered *Kirtanas*. He said, had he met Bhaurao before, he would have started his work. He would have been his companion in education work. In fact, he thought that it was his work. Mukadam Tatya of Kusur came in the main stream work of the Sanstha because of Baba (Gadage Maharaj). Tatya became a full time life worker of the Sanstha. Bhaurao said in 1954, "I'm going to start a college at Karad and it will be named after the modern saint of Maharashtra, Sant Gadage Maharaj." People were shocked to hear the announcement of Bhaurao.

One activist asked, "Anna how is it possible to start a college at Karad? You know, how difficult it is to start a college."

Bhaurao said, "See, I always make an announcement of a good work well in advance and after that I set myself behind it like a missionary person. This is how I work and that gives me satisfaction."

"But Anna, there is a question of money; we've no funds. First, we must make arrangements for funds and then only we must announce".

"See my boy, when we make announcements publicly, it naturally compels us to carry the work. It becomes our moral responsibility to work out the plan. So now, I have to keep my words. I cannot keep the work incomplete. You'll see now I'll complete the work.

Mukadam Tatya donated one lakh rupees. The application was forwarded to the university. The commission visited the site and the permission to start the college was also granted. Barrister P. G. Patil curiously asked the Principal Suru, one of the members of the commission that how the commission granted permission to start a college at Karad where there was no infrastructure, no building. There was only a sort of dismantled shed like structure standing on the open space. Principal Suru said, "We did not see building of stones and bricks but we saw great people involved in the process and who would say *no* to Bhaurao Patil's college."

Bhaurao collected donations from everywhere. He toured Pune city. He called Mayer of Pune, Shankarrao Urasal. He called the other activists like Dnyanoba Jadhav, Namdevrao Mate. They wandered the city. Bhaurao visited the famous *Mandai* (the Market place) of Pune. He appealed to people to donate one day's income to him. He got extemporaneous response from people. He told them that this college was for the children of workers and farmers. If they seek education here, they will never forget your contributions.

There was a wonderful response to his speech. From a collie to woman sweepers of the Mandai, all people gave donations ranging from four annas to one rupee and 500 to 1000 rupees from the rich. The poor people wished to get connected to the Sanstha through their donations. Bhaurao thought that this sense of belonging of the poor was more important factor to him. His Sanstha was not a manifestation of personal achievement but it was a social transformation of his times.

He deposited the amount in the university. Dr. Dhananjayrao Gadgil said on this occasion that Pune had a reputation of collecting funds from all over the world, but it was unheard that an outsider visited Pune and succeeded in collecting funds. Bhaurao did what seemed impossible to a non-Puneit.

On the occasion of the inaugural function of this college, donors from Pune Mandai in a special bus came to Karad to attend the function. Dr. Gadgil and Bhaurao admired and appreciated the participation of the people.

Bhaurao and Gadage Maharaj had a strong wish to start a college at Pandharpur, the holy place of Maharashtra, and it was done. With support and financial assistance of R. B. Borawake and Dakale, colleges were also started at Shrirampur. An engineering college was also started at Satara at the same juncture of time.

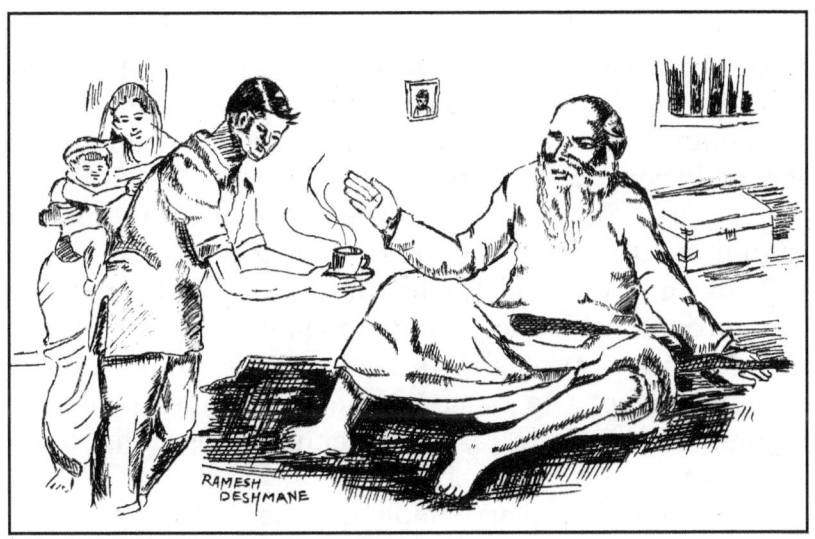

34

There have been innumerable people in Maharashtra who have spent their entire life for the country. There have been also no dearths of activists who have devoted their entire life for social transformation and served the country till their last breath. Similarly, with the help of power many have contributed in the social work, however such people develop a habit to live in a halo of sacrifice that they have done. They gradually change concepts of their own individuality. Later, in course of time due to the enhanced financial status, their thinking and attitudes change. Some of them get into a trap of selfish ends and they promote their children and kith and kins. Some develop into egoist personalities and prefer to live in their own halo and whim. Flattering sycophants surround them tempting them a life of self-pride and egoism. They subsequently expect people to recognize them in high sounding terms.

However, all social workers do not develop similar kind of ego and whim. There had been a race of ideal leaders and thinkers that Maharashtra has produced like Maharshi Karve, Dr. Babasaheb Ambedkar, Vitthal Ramaji Shinde, Vinobaji Bhave etc. Karmveer Bhaurao Patil belonged to this group. As an activist, Bhaurao's work was undoubtedly immense and breathtaking but as a human being he was even greater than that. It is indeed beyond description.

Man is often known by his actions, his work and his commitment to his work. Bhaurao categorically refused to lead an elitist and luxury life. He did not have any temptations, selfish ends and personal ambitions. So, he did not have any desire to lead a life of comfort as it usually happens to those people who amass a certain amount of fortune in terms of wealth, recognition, fame and name.

Bhaurao led a very simple life like that of a common man of his region. Historically speaking, Bhaurao's work in the realm of education is fundamental. It is a massive contribution in the cultural history of Maharashtra during the twentieth century. However, his humanistic approach with which he handled odds in quaint journey of his work was strikingly different.

Bhaurao hailed from Sangli district. The name of his village is Aitawade. He had his home at the village. But he gave it up. He never turned to his home. His house collapsed in course of time. The people stole whatever they found there. Later his neighbors snatched his home. He had a few acres of land which he donated to the Sanstha.

He lived in Satara most of the time but he did not have his home in Satara too. All his life, he lived at a rented place. With a very humble beginning of the Sanstha, he lived in a shed and hut like structure with his boys. In course of time, he got hundreds of acres of land in donation form, but he did not use a piece of a land for his personal purpose. Such a thought never occured to his mind. People donated lakhs of rupees, buildings to the Sanstha, but he never took a single paisa from it. He used the entire funds for the Sanstha and submitted accounts to the Sanstha. When he was on a tour and travelled extensively, he spent money which was required to be spent. He submitted details of donations to the Sanstha office. Donations given to the Sanstha must be spent for development of the Sanstha only; this was his approach. People donate their hard earned money for education of the poor. If you use such funds for personal purposes, it would be a blunder and a social crime. So, he was very sensitive about such matters. He took care to carry a required amount only while he was on tours. He submitted details of travel expenditures and donations to the Sanstha accountant. Once, it happened that Bhaurao was on tour in Sangli region and the Nehru shirt that he was wearing was overused. Its pocket had a hole in it which Bhaurao did not notice. The coins that he had kept in the pocket were dropped. When he sat down to present the account details, he found that he was short of one rupee and six annas. He recalled details of the money he spent. He checked and checked the details but the figure came the same. Later, he saw that his pocket had a hole and the coins had been dropped. He told the student secretary (the accountant), "See my boy, I'm not in a position to give you details about one rupee and six annas. Perhaps, some coins had been dropped through the hole of my pocket. I did not realize it. You minus the amount, when you give me money for the next tour." The student-accountant wondered and kept looking on at him for some time. He was confused. For a moment, image of Saint Eknath appeared in his eyes. Saint Eknath could not sleep a wink all night because he could not tally a day's expenditures.

Former students of the Sanstha sent some amount from their salaries to Bhaurao. Bhaurao called it *Gurudakshina*. Later, he produced a fund called Laxmibai Patil Fund in memory of his wife. He gave loans to the poor students without interest. The principle was that after completion of education, students returned their loans. It was an innovative banking experiment in an era when no such loans were even thought of. Students of the Sanstha helped the upcoming new generation. Bhaurao took sixty rupees per month for his personal expenses from the fund. Many activists and distinguished persons visited the Sanstha. At times, they stayed at his residence. But he maintained his expenses in a meager amount given to him. His son and daughter in-law also did not complain.

Basically, this was the outcome of the Gurudakshina Fund. Bhaurao had absolute moral standing to borrow more funds but he was reluctant to do it. He was categorical about his personal expenses. He told his accountant to write down details of his withdrawals, so that he could return it whenever it was possible.

Bhaurao started the Sanstha by depositing six thousand rupees. He sold eighty to ninety hundred gram gold that his wife possessed. This was the event of 1926-27. If Bhaurao had claimed the amount, no one might have objected. And it was his moral claim. But he never did anything of that sort. On the contrary, he felt guilty for withdrawing sixty rupees per month for his personal expenses. He wished strongly to return the same. Once, Marutrao Katkar, the Sanstha activist was having tea at his residence. He saw that the cup he was using had several cracks. Katkar said, "Anna, I'll buy a new set of cup and saucers for you, they are always wanted in the home". Bhaurao reacted, "See, if that is possible in our monthly budget." He was very particular about household expenditures.

What are today's state of affairs of so called education barons? Today's educational barons draw huge donations and live posh life. On this background, one can see Bhaurao's sacrifice and commitment to his work. He took education to the poor and downtrodden communities of Maharashtra.

Bhaurao sacrificed his entire personal possessions including his wife's golden ornaments for the Sanstha. At the same time, he did not hesitate to snatch as much as gold from his kith and kins and even relatives. Once, his daughter came to see him; she was married and was with her husband in Sangli. Bhaurao was in financial difficulties. He wanted to pay fees of the college going girls of his boarding. His eyes fell on his daughter's golden bangles. He said intentionally that her bangles were thin enough and they did not suit her status. He told her that he'll return her bangles by adding more gold and make them thick enough. Bhaurao literally snatched her bangles and spent them for college fees of boarding girls. Of course, he never returned them to his daughter. She also never asked for her bangles

Bhaurao travelled a lot for donations. But he never stayed at expensive hotels. He preferred to stay at residences of his friends. When he was in Pune, he stayed at the residence of Bhaurao Sanas. Sometimes, he stayed at Hotel Samadhan but the owner never charged him. He stayed at Bharat Lodge of Agrwal in Mahabaleshwar.

The hotel owner respected Bhaurao so much so that he did not charge him. At Wai, he stayed at Missionary Hospital where his friends paid his bills. He took a lot of care that his personal expenses did not tax the Sanstha.

Bhaurao followed certain principles in his personal life. He was a follower of Mahatma Gandhiji. He had reduced most of his personal needs. He had a few Khadhi Nehru shirts and two three *panchas*. He never used handkerchiefs. His never got his clothes ironed. He used Nehru shirts made from the cloth produced by the boarding boys. He used dhoti made by his boys. His bedding materials were simple. Boys from Astha School gave him *jeens* and a similar type of *ghongadi*. He used it as his bedding. He used the same clothes on all occasions even in ceremonies, Sanstha meetings or during his farm visits or his long journey. He never gave undue importance to such superfluous outer coverings. During cold seasons, he used jackets.

From 1919 onwards, he never used shoes and his head was always unprotected. He never shaved. So his beard grew longer and rested it up to his belly. His head was bald in its central place, so the side hair of his head mixed in his white beard. He held a country made stick in his hand. His meals were simple. He drank butter milk; he ate groundnuts, onion, chutney and bhakari. It was a rural based food. So he never had any problems when he visited villages or far off Wadi-vastis.

Bhaurao was secular. He never performed religions rites. All his life, he worked for untouchables and depressed communities. He never observed any fasting day. He never followed any diet. Once, Bhaurao's driver was not ready to eat anything as he was observing a fasting day. Bhaurao said, "Arre, Uddhav, there is no fasting day for people like us; we eat as long as we get food and when we don't get anything, that is our fasting day." And he got up to eat his meals. He also took the driver with him. If there are no differences in eating dishes then why should we follow discriminations with whom we sit for eating; he said. He forced the driver to eat meals with him.

Once, he was on tour in Koregaon region. He stayed at the residence of some acquaintance. There was a farmer and his wife in the home. Bhaurao heard some whispering between wife and husband about what could be cooked when there was nothing to be cooked in the home. The couple was poor; they did not have money either. Bhaurao was very sensitive in such matters. He called them out and said, "See my brother; I haven't come for tea or any kind of hospitability here."

"How do you say so Anna? A person like you visiting our home and...?

"What do you have in your home?"

"Nothing Anna; no sugar no tea powder", the man said humiliatingly.

"Don't you have groundnuts?"

"Yes, I have."

"And jaggery?", Bhaurao asked.

"Lot of!" the man said excitedly.

"Then you do one thing, take two fistful of groundnut and a piece of jaggery and bring a glass of water from the earthen pitcher. Why are you scared? That's the hospitability."

"Yes, I'll do it immediately", said the man literally running inside his home.

Bhaurao called him back. "See my son, I'll do this on one condition; you must do something for my boarding boys as per your capacity. This is not good to eat groundnuts and jaggery here when my boys are hungry there."

"Yes, Anna, I'll give something but first you eat; giving something to you is a holy work."

Bhaurao ate groundnuts and jaggery. At some

places, he only drank butter-milk. He developed such habits that suited his innumerable poor donors. The habits which he found troublesome to his donors, he gave them up. The anecdote about the habit of tea is a memorable. Bhaurao never used to drink tea. He was habituated to drink milk. If milk was not available, he preferred water but never tea. But how could a poor man be happy by only giving water to Bhaurao? Can drinking a glass of water be hospitability?

Once, Bhaurao was in Mumbai. As he was walking along the footpath in Lalbag, a former student of the Sanstha met him. After routine inquiries and whereabouts, the student wholeheartedly invited Bhaurao to his home.

He said, "I stay here at a short distance. Anna you must visit my home." Bhaurao could say *no* to the Sanstha student. He reached his home. What a home! It was just a home of one room and a big curtain dividing the room into two parts. Bhaurao sat in one of the parts of the room and the boy went inside and said to his wife, "Give a cup of milk, Anna dose not drink tea."

The wife replied, "Where from you picked this bearded man? Where from I can bring milk? There is a little milk left and if that is given to this bearded man, how can I feed my child?" The couple was whispering behind the curtain and Bhaurao heard it effortlessly. The student brought a cup of milk for Bhaurao after some moments when he said to the boy, "Arre, I haven't come to you to drink milk. I'll drink tea in your home." The boy felt humiliated and became speechless. When his wife come forward and said, "Excuse me if I have done anything wrong, don't take my words to your heart Anna."

Bhaurao said, "No no, my girl, nothing has gone wrong; you haven't done anything wrong. On the contrary, you have taught me something. It never occurred to me that our likes and dislike bring people into troubles for no fault of their own. Nobody spoke like you so directly. But I understand there must be same situation in every home. I did not realize it till this moment. Today, I understand my mistake. I must change. I'll start drinking tea from today."

Bhaurao started drinking tea whenever he visited poor donors. There are people who look forward for luxurious hospitability from others and here was a person who was worried about troubles of his donors and hosts. He thought that one's behavior must be such that it should not trouble others.

The garden at Dhanini's Baug was full of fruits. There were coconuts, papaya. mango trees, and vegetables. Bhaurao sold fruit and agro-products in the market and the money he got was used for boarding expenses. There were buffaloes in the campus and there was enough milk. But he never took anything from it for his personal use. He said, "You need to buy these things from market and pay money, so why not pay money to the Sanstha?" But he did not do it consciously because people might suspect that he was using the Sanstha as a personal access. So he bought things from market at times paying more.

Once, Bhaurao's son Appasaheb had been to Kolhapur. So he visited the branch of the Sanstha at Rukadi near Kolhapur. He brought with him a sack of groundnuts while returning home. Of course, he paid the bill. But Bhaurao became very angry. He said, "First, you send the sack back to the branch and bring back the money you paid. Because the person whom you paid the bill knows only that you paid the bill. The others might think that you got it as a free gift from the branch. People should not raise their fingers at us and we must take care of it." Appasaheb later returned the sack to the Rukadi branch. In such situations, people crosscheck your private face. Bhaurao was a transparent person and so was his greatness! So he never did any such kinds of things even in his day-today life.

Broadly speaking, Bhaurao had little interest in familial matters. He did take part in familial matters but he was more interested in family matters of his students. He had two sons and a daughter. The name of his elderly son is Appasaheb and the daughter's name is Shakuntala. As father he did not do much for them. His son Appasaheb took education with boarding boys. After completion of his education, he got employment in the Sanstha. It was an easy access to employment for his family people. But Bhaurao persuaded his son not to do so in the Sanstha. He advised him to join Insurance Company.

Walchand Shet, an industrialist had started a factory in Bangalore and Appasaheb requested his father to give a letter of recommendation so that he might get the job. The industrialist had a soft corner for the Jain community. Bhaurao was a Jain. Appasaheb thought that there was some space for him to get the job in Bangalore. But Bhaurao refused to give him any such casteial recommendation. He did not believe in favouritism. He was against such practice. He thought that one must go by one's performance, qualifications, accountability and hard work. But Bhaurao gave hundreds of such recommendation letters to his able students. Any father in his place would have granted the wish of his son. He was to give him only a letter of recommendation. But Bhaurao did not do it. He told his son, "Appa, you ask me anything but not a letter of recommendation, It might mean that I'm using my influence for you." Bhaurao did not do much for his son. But he did a lot for children of the Sanstha activists. He wrote hundreds of letters. Once, while he was going to Devapur, he took a short halt at Waduj. He stayed at Rambhau Nalawade's home. Nalawade's younger daughter was found of fish. She requested Bhaurao to bring at least one fish from Rajewadi Lake. Bhaurao was a Jain and a strict vegetarian. Still he stopped at the lake and got a fish for Nalawade's daughter. But he did not do much for his family and the people.

Selflessness was his virtue. He was a man of principles. He never entertained members of his family or relatives; in the sense to give them jobs when they did not possess required qualifications. This was the ideal of Bhaurao's personality. It set down a standard of morality. It shows to what extent one can stretch one's principled behaviour to prove one's ability to stand firm in times of crisis. Such an example of ideal personality in today's social, cultural and political era is rare.

Bhaurao's younger brother Balawantrao after retiring from the government job thought of joining the Sanstha as Superintendent in Chhatrapati Shahu Boarding without taking even any honorarium. But Bhaurao did not give him permission. He never allowed anyone to have an advantage of suspicion. He believed firmly that the Sanstha belonged to the people. It was raised out of the contributions, donations and blessings of people. So, he never wanted anyone to suspect that he was taking disadvantage of the Sanstha by pushing his people into it. He was very particular about it till his death.

In a letter addressed to his son in 1954, he writes: "I am aware that I've not done anything for you as any father might do. What we did as parents? We gave you birth and brought you in this world. I also snatched your mother's *Mangalsutra* and used it for education of the poor. Your mother supported me all her life in my mission. She breathed her last serving the Sanstha. So remember my son, you are a child of such parents. They lived entirely for others. You too must sacrifice and work for the poor. Remember your happiness must always lie in happiness of others."

"I always wished that you should never do any job in the Sanstha. The store where you were working last year was in loss. There are no chances in future that the store will do well. So, the Sanstha is planning to retrench its employees. In such situation, how the store management will retrench you? Besides, you are my son. So naturally, others were retrenched in place of you. You start a job on your own. You go for Insurance Company. If you make efforts to stand independently, you will be happy. You will get satisfaction in your life. It is true that you have not received any support or assistance from your father. And remember; in future also don't hope for any such concessions. You must moreover look after my mother. She is at Aitawade. I'll give you a few acres of land at the village. You can draw about 300 to 500 rupees as yearly income. In future, if I too fall sick, you have to take care of me too and spend money on me from your income."

What does this letter show? Bhaurao was very transparent in his personal life. He had no two faces. His public and private life was the same. He did not hide anything. Such was his character. Truth, sacrifice, character, principled moral behavior were his rich possessions. He never succumbed to any temptations. He never made compromises that came in his ways.

Bhaurao gave importance to the principle of dignity of labour. He did what he said. He himself participated in a number of tasks of the Sanstha like cleaning latrines of Shivaji College, making roads in villages like Budhagaon, Kolhapur, Sangli, etc.

The government recognized his work and sent a letter granting him 300 rupees per month as honorarium. Bhaurao returned the proposal to the government. He wrote a letter to the government. He writes in the letter: "My efforts are directed in the sense that the people in Hindustan should live as integrated society respecting principle of humanism. The people should work in this light to establish such principles in our country. It is a national task. I am devoting my life for this mission. I never expected that I will be getting some monetary gain for such tasks. So, I do not wish to accept your honorarium and I feel regretful for the same."

Bhaurao's letter throws light on his unique personality. He thought that the social work of his stature should not be valued in terms of money. Similarly, by accepting such honorarium, one gets obliged to someone who pays for your work. Subsequently, you are brought under pressure. Your freedom is lost. Bhaurao did not want such kinds of obligations. He served society selflessly without expectations. He never wore hypocritical and superfluous masks. He was crystal clear of want he was doing and what he aspired for. This perception is very important in today's times.

Once, he had been to Ninam-Padali, a village place near Satara town. He moved from door to door and accumulated whatever assistance he collected. He was engrossed in his work so much so that he did not even realize when darkness fell all around him. Suddenly, the sky became dark. Bhaurao was afraid because he did not wish to oscillate between the heavy rain and darkness. He lifted hastily the heavy bundle on his head and started walking. A villager came to his help. He divided the bundle in two parts and held one on his head. They covered half the distance. But terrific lightening and darkness engulfed them. They could not see anything not even the road. It started raining heavily. The muddled road was full of thorns; it made their journey difficult. Bhaurao had given up wearing shoes long back. His feet were of thorns. The man accompanying him said, "Anna, now listen to me, put on my shoes; nobody will see you in darkness that you have broken your pledge." Bhaurao said, "I do not follow the pledge for others. I follow it for myself." The next day, Bhaurao's feet was swollen. All day, he wrestled to get thorns out of his feet. It became extremely difficult for him to walk for a couple of days. Bhaurao never gave up his principles. Similarly, he never brought imbalance between his thoughts and behavior.

Bhaurao's personality was composed of such rich traits highlighting his ideology. He was a very simple man like any other common person. Sometimes, he neglected the other even if they were misbehaving. Sometimes, he burst out in anger. Sometimes he abused in slang. He neglected boys if they were going for a movie. But his eyes were sharp enough on his boys. He did not want them get into trap of any addictions. The school and college going boys visited hotels and cinema theatres. They were afraid of Bhaurao but they managed. He did not hush them up if they went to cinema. He carried necessary food-items for his boys who were studying in different colleges.

Once, he was nearing the Union Boarding in Pune. The boys saw him coming and ran away in fear. One boy came near to him, "Give it to me Anna!"

"Why my lad, you didn't go to the cinema." The boy was shocked. He did not understand for some time how Bhaurao identified that some boys had been to cinema.

He said, 'No, I did not go."

"All right, but if you feel like going, you should go." Bhaurao said while walking with the boy.

Simplicity, unbound selflessness and love for his boys had been his ideals all his life. He was a true activist. So, he was able to follow extraordinary principled life. He always remained away from vices. Such unbelieving capability and spiritual strength only a person like Bhaurao can possess. We are indeed perplexed to know that a person like Bhaurao Patil really lived and walked in the hilly and barren regions of Maharashtra.

Bhaurao consistently worked for more than twenty four years. He faced all odds that came in his way. He overcame them and achieved what he was aspiring for. He never gave up though he encountered impasse situations. He pursued his work patiently. He never blamed others and the society. He was therefore never frustrated. He produced an army of committed activities. They sought education in his Sanstha. The same army accompanied him in his works. They took an oath in his name and remained true to their words. In course of time his works got social and cultural recognition. He received support from all corners of the society.

Maharshi Vitthal Ramaji Shinde addressed his students who took an oath in his name. Shinde said, "The social work is like a walnut tree. The person who plants it, he never gets opportunity to taste its fruits. But Bhaurao, you are a fortunate person. You are getting the fruits of your work in your own life time." This was how peoples' attitudes and perception towards his work changed. Educationists admired his work wholeheartedly. The society at large recognized his work. Bhaurao was rendering difficult and precious work. As his works got recognition, people organized several functions to felicitate him. People offered him *Nidhis*.

They wanted to participate in the works that he was engaged in. There was a sort of a competition among people to give him more and more Nidhis.

Bhaurao opened a school in Kirloskarwadi. Once upon a time, he had worked in the Kirloskar Company. The workers came together and offered a Nidhi of twenty five thousand rupees. The function took place at Kirloskarwadi. The central minister D. P. Karmarkar presided over. The merchants of Kolhapur conducted a similar kind of function and handed over him a Nidhi of twenty five thousand rupees. Malojirao Nimbalkar of Phaltan felicitated him in in his *Darabar* and gave him a Nidhi of ten thousand rupees. Satara Local Board (today's Zilla Parishad) felicitated him. It was a huge programme. Bhai Madhavrao Bagal of Kolhapur and Krantisinh Nana Patil were invited for this programme. They were also felicitated for their contribution in their respective fields. Bhaurao was sick and his health was not good still he attended the function.

He spoke on this occasion. What Bhaurao said on this occasion shows his prophetic attitudes. He said, "I never looked at anyone as my *Guru*. But I believe in the works of a few persons like our great historical hero Chhatrapati Shivaji Maharaj, Rajarshi Shahu Maharaj, Mahatma Jyotiba Phule, Vitthal Ramaji Shinde, Dr. Babasaheb Ambedkar, Gadgebaba and Mahatma Gandhi. These were my inspirational forces. Their works gave me spiritual strength and energy. It is true that I have criticized the Brahmin community. But, today the time has come that we must bury such discriminations. There is no meaning to delve into the past.. What is important is huge and mammoth tasks that lie before us. We must produce activists to make our society better. We have to devote all our life for this great task. In Pune, the educational institutions like Deccan Education Society and Dhondo Keshav Karve attempted great works. With missionary zeal, they worked hard and set down standards in Maharashtra. We must follow their ideals.

Bhaurao's students of Satara district came together. They founded student's congress committee to collect a fund of one lakh rupees to donate to the Sanstha. The committee organized a programme to felicitate him. The students wanted Mahatma Gandhi to attend the programme and felicitate Bhaurao. So they met Bapuji. Mahatma Gandhi said, "You're doing a great work! Felicitation of Bhaurao's works is a praiseworthy event. I personally would love to attend it but the Hindu-Muslim riots have triggered anarchy in our country. Situations compel me to tour Pakistan. So I feel regretful that I won't be able to attend the programme."

The student congress later invited Sant Gadgebaba. He was also on the Karnataka tour. But he postponed his programme and agreed to attend Bhaurao's felicitation. It appeared to him that Bhaurao's felicitation was more important than his tour. The birth anniversary of Mahatma Phule in 1948 was fixed as the programme date. A procession was organized in Satara starting from Dhanini's Baug. An elephant from Chhatrapati's palace was arranged. The students insisted Bhaurao to sit on the elephant. Bhaurao said, "Talk to Baba, seek his permission and request him to sit on the elephant." Baba said to Bhaurao, "You sit on the elephant, I won't." Somebody again requested Baba. He said, "It seems he wants to sit, so tell him to sit, today is his day." But neither Bhaurao nor Baba sat on the elephant.

About twenty thousand people attended the programme. The students' congress presented to Bhaurao one lack one thousand one hundred and eleven rupees Nidhi and a memorandum in admiration of his work. He spoke on this occasion. His said, "I had a strong wish that if Mahatma Gandhi would not find time to attend this programme, Baba must attend it and Baba came all away from Mysore for the function. It shows his love towards the Sanstha and me. Vitthal (God) is not just in Pandharpur; he resides in every one of us. This is a lesson that Baba has taught us. Seeds of democracy lie in mass education. Education though self-help is my motto. It is a *yugdharma*. If people are illiterate, there will be anarchy. I am educating masses to put an end to discriminations and religious and casteial walls. We will produce leaders of tomorrow from masses only. Mass leaders will understand problems and difficulties of people. My schools will educate them. I said that I will open 101 high schools in the name of Mahatma Gandhiji. I also plan to start a university called Mahatma Gandhi Gramin University. You are doing great favour to me by giving funds for the Sanstha. I'll repay you by doing all possible works for society."

Baba said, "I served people and helped them to become good human beings but Bhaurao turned stones into godly figures. He tills land and serves the black mother. By opening new schools, he serves the poor and educates them. He is responsible for producing an army of educated people. They'll serve the nation. So, his works are immense."

The government meanwhile stopped the grants of the Sanstha. This obviously brought Bhaurao in a financial disaster. But the funds in the name of his felicitation programmes boosted his morale and he pursued his work patiently.

The next day another programme was organized. This was a ceremony of gratitude and his students organized it. To run such a huge institution, huge funds were necessary. Bhaurao wandered like a mad person for funds. All his life, he travelled to collect funds and suffered greatly simply for collecting funds. He did not use shoes all his life. So the students decided to give him a motor car. Bhaurao was against such a plan. Earlier, Malojirao Naik Nimbalkar had proposed to give him a car but he opposed it. Later, Ramchandrarao Pawar and Tadaskar Bhaurao's friends wanted to give him a car but he again opposed. Now in his old age, he needed his own vehicle to travel extensively. His students thought so. They persuaded him that they were not doing a favour to him but performing a duty as son would do to his father. They promised him that they will pay for petrol and driver's salaries. This burden will not be put on the Sanstha. Bhaurao was somehow prepared to accept the gift. The programme was organized on 18 November 1948. A huge crowd of students attended it.

Many students spoke on this occasion. They told Bhaurao not to join politics. The people who attended the programme spread a wrong word among the public that Bhaurao was going to join politics. Dhimate, his student came forward courageously and said, "Anna, you travel a lot, you suffered for us, now you must accept our gift and you are not going to join politics." Another student spoke in the same way. Then, Bhaurao stood up; his face was writhing in anger. He said, "Yes, it is true that I criticized the CM, Balasaheb Kher but that was not the personal criticism. It was a representative feeling of the society. All my life I fought against injustice. My motto is 'love for justice and hatred for injustice.' My students are those who look at offence as offence. And you give me a motor-gift so that I must get obliged. Was there a motor car with me till today? And who are you to teach me? Who are you to advise me whether to join politics or not? I will never give up politics. On the contrary, I will always participate in politics whenever there is injustice. I have resigned the Sanstha work long back." Bhaurao's eyes were writhing in fire and tears simultaneously. He was terribly upset. He was sweating. He was breathing fast.

Who is god for us? Or whom we call god? Is He a person in whom we do not find weakness and limitations that we find in man? Is He someone who follows ideals and walks down His life with principles? Is He someone who does not look at His own personal needs and wants? Do we consider such a person a godly person?

Bhaurao was a hot tempered man however he cooled down soon; or he was a godly person. In his day today works, he was came in contact with innumerable people. He was a godly person who never had faith in existence of god. Once Bhaurao accepted someone, he would accept him in absolute sense. He took care of boarding boys and their families too. He looked into family problems of boys as his personal problems. So he often met parents and sorted out problems. Every boy from boarding was his son and Bhaurao was his father. Difficulties of their families were his difficulties. He was a fatherly person to every student. He considered every student as his family member.

Once, his student, Keshavrao Pawar's father passed away. He was in the eleventh standard then. Bhaurao felt very sad for his student. Keshavrao had a married sister, a younger brother, some cattle and a few acres of land dependent on the rains. After the death of his father,

Keshavrao had to shoulder family responsibilities. So, he decided to give up education. Bhaurao wrote to him: "Send your sister to her husband and bring your young brother in the boarding. I'll teach your brother." He took the entire responsibilities of the family. He gave him fatherly support. It was because of him, Keshavrao completed his education. Later Keshavrao became an advocate and remained true to him and the Sanstha. He said, "Anna supported me as father; had he not given me support, I would have been running behind the cattle waywardly playing with their tails."

For Bhaurao, Barrister P.G.Patil was like his son. When Barrister Patil was abroad, he sent fifteen rupees money order to his grandmother every month. He visited Kawalapur frequently, Barrister Patil's village to meet his grandmother. He also met Mr. Patil's sisters at his residence. When he returned from Sangli, he handed over to his driver a saree and a piece of cloth for his sister. He did not give such gifts to his children or even to his grandchildren. There are similar examples with persons like Principal M. A. Swami and Principal Narayanrao Bhagare. Principal Swami's old mother was staying at Shivade village. Bhaurao had sent Mr. Swami to Varanasi for higher education. He sent money for his education per month and he did not forget to send fifteen rupees per month to his mother. If he was touring in the region, he did not forget to pay a visit and modestly do whatever was possible for them.

Principal Bhagare's situation was worse than Swami. His widowed mother brought him up in critical conditions. When Bhagare came in the boarding, he took care of his mother. He looked at her as his sister. He spent money on her medical needs. He asked the Sanstha administration to spend money. Bhaurao not only looked after his students but also their families.

Besides, he took initiatives in arranging marriages

of his students He gave valuable tips as to what type of bride might suit to his students. During marriage ceremonies, his behaviour in bride grooms home was as if it were his own home. He gave detailed tips as how to shoulder family responsibilities and to carry out financial commitments. Where to keep a sack of coal in bathroom and were should be a kerosene tin. If a married bride was illiterate or had given up education, he encouraged her to pursue her studies. He would also give her a good job. Barrister P. G. Patil's wife Sumati Patil was a graduate. Bhaurao took initiatives and persuaded her to complete post graduate education in English. Later, she worked as a lecturer in English and also as the Principal of Shivaji College. She retired as the Chairperson of MPSC. (Maharashtra Public Servile Commission)

Bhaurao came in close contact with Kanase family from Dahiwadi. Mr. Kanase was a government servant and he wanted his children to pursue higher studies. But his unfavorable financial conditions could not allow him to do so. Bhaurao provided them jobs in the Sanstha. He thus made such arrangements for innumerable rural children of Maharashtra and promoted them for higher studies.

In Astha School, G. T. Joshi, a Brahmin head-master faced difficulties as the villagers demanded a non-Brahmin head-master. But Bhaurao had no caste prejudices. He did not change his decision only because of the whims of the villagers of Astha. Once, he was wandering in the farm side near the school campus. He found a large-sized gourd fruit. He carried it and gave it to the head-master Mr. Joshi. He said, "This is the first gift to you on behalf of the Sanstha. You have to carry it with your own hands up to your home." Bhaurao did it because Mr. Joshi was weak and bony man. But he was a very good teacher. He wanted to tone down the tension of Mr. Joshi. He helped him in all respects and finally the people of Astha were happy when they understood Bhaurao's right attitudes.

The love and trust that he possessed for his employees, made them to work for the Sanstha though many of them were paid poorly. Bhaurao gave his employees vegetables that were produced in the Sanstha farms. He would give them the eatables that he had in his home as a part of hospitability. That was why, his employees were happy to work. He was like a huge tree giving them cool shadows in the scorching sunlight. As the rains give water and the sun provides light to everyone; as the river offers life selflessly to all bushes and trees, Bhaurao gave everything to his students. He treated everyone with a sense of equality. So a person like Bhaurao must be included in the tradition of great historical heroes.

Bhaurao always said that he did not first go for long term plans. He knew it that they evolve as requirements come across in course of time. The Sanstha grew gradually; its expansion went with scores of difficulties. The Sanstha helped to establish boarding and more branches at different places. It opened schools and then colleges. With expansion, teaching and non-teaching staff increased. Teachers were not paid good salaries in the past. Naturally, they had to go through several problems. Particularly in such situations to meet medical expenses or some such other needs, they were in financial problems. Bhaurao identified the need of his staff and he started Rayat Sevak Co-operative Society. It was later on transformed into a bank. The Sanstha staff got a funding agency of their own and they resolved their financial problems. Besides, the staff saved their hard earned money as bank deposits. Today this bank's transactions are in crores of rupees.

Students who came from rural regions always faced problems of funds. Rural boys came to stay at the Sanstha boarding. They were always in need of some funds for their education. Bhaurao made separate arrangements to fulfill such demands of needy students. He started a fund for this specific purpose in the name of his wife. It was called Laxmibai Patil Fund. The fund sanctioned educational loans to the needy students without charging any interest on the loans. The students paid the loan after they got jobs in future. The staff of the Sanstha donated some amount for this fund. Later, this fund was registered and as per the government norms two percent interest was incurred on the loan.

Similarly, one more Sevak Welfare Fund was started to provide financial assistance to the staff in times of emergencies, crucial medical treatments and sudden deaths. The Sanstha started periodicals like *Rayat Sevak* and *Rayat Shikshan Patrika* to enlighten on various issues and help student community to equip with latest tools to update them in today's globalized world. Karmveer Vidya Prabodhini was established in 1974 to achieve multi-sided developments of student community. The agricultural department of the Sanstha did several experiments. New departments were opened to provide professional and technical training to the students. A useful training centre was started at Dahiwadi to provide special training to the shepherd community. Today the Government of Maharashtra administers the centre. The Sanstha started a printing press. The Sanstha is rendering various services at different centres to inculcate values among students. Besides, the Sanstha is taking efforts in starting pre-primary schools. Some of the projects have been started by Bhaurao himself and he took maximum efforts in implementing many of them. A number of projects Bhaurao planned in his life-time but due to several problems, he could not complete them. But later the life members of the Sanstha completed them. The projects achieved social and cultural reformation of the society. The projects highlight the principle, of *Bhaujan Hitay Bahujan Sukhay*. That is social happiness lies in social welfare.

Bhaurao made education a means and also an end in itself. He looked at it as a powerful tool of social change. He simultaneously wanted an individual to achieve personal and social enrichment. He therefore went for varied experimentations. He visualized that individuals must inculcate such virtues among themselves. And he was successful in connecting education to life.

Similarly, he wanted to put an end to social disorder, evil customs and traditions prevalent in the society. He used education as a powerful tool. That is why, Bhaurao was not only an educationist but he was equally a significant social revolutionary. His social work is therefore equally important like his contributions in education. He longed to develop excellence in society all his life. He wanted to end social evils. For him, society was his god and education was its worship.

He worked for social change. He never believed in casteial attitudes. Similarly, he did not believe in religion. His religion was humanism. He started his boarding with a Harijan boy. Students belonging to different castes and religion were in his boarding. They lived under a single roof. They ate and slept at one place. It was an unusual experiment in social and educational field. Even Bhaurao's Guru, Shahu Maharaj could not succeed in it. Bhaurao overcame limitations of his Guru. He defeated his Guru. It was an admirable defeat. He went a step ahead.

The government took cognizance and admired his attempts of eradicating untouchability. Harijan Sevak Sangh took cognizance of his works. Bhaurao followed a simple principle; he first attempted tasks and then he talked about it. Once, the Harijan community organized programme at Palus, a village near Sangli. Bhaurao addressed the audience. A friend of him from Satara, Saradar Dadasaheb Panditrao accompanied him. He ate with the Harijan people after the meeting. He made his friend to eat with the Harijan. He never observed caste discriminations all his life.

The period in which Bhaurao worked was unfavourable for such ventures. The problem of untouchability was sensitive among Savarna people. They did not touch the Harijans. They kept considerable distance from them. They took care that even their shadows should not fall on them. They gave them stale food. While giving food, they took care that they would not touch them. They were given hard tasks. They pulled dead animals and peeled their skins. Such were the social traditions and customs; this was our culture. So, the Harijans went through harassment and social turmoil. Even educated untouchables faced such evils. Bhaurao himself saw that educated Harijan boys were facing such discriminations. He sent a young Mahar as head-master in Astha School. His name was Khairmode. People of Astha said that they would not accept a Mahar head-master. But he did not grant their demand. But Mr. Khairmode took pains and worked hard. Because of his efforts, the school improved rapidly. The results of the school excelled up to 95 percent. Bhaurao was obviously happy about his brilliant performance. In one meeting conducted in Astha, he admired the efforts of Khairmode. But unfortunately Khairmode died of tuberculosis in a short time and it was a shock to Bhaurao.

Bhaurao always supported the Harijans and bahujan communities. He stood behind the Brahmin community as well. He had no prejudices against them. Some Brahmins misunderstood him and they thought that he was against them. He had innumerable Brahmin friends and well-wishers. There were many Brahmin activists, teachers, office bearers in the Sanstha. The Brahmins like R. B. Kale, the playwright, Gupte, Dhanjayrao Gadgil, Sardar Panditrao, Gajendragadkar, Acharya Atre, Sane Guruji, S. M. Mate, Balasaheb Kher, Maharshi Karve, Wrangler Paranjpe, Mahajani and Principal Suru were his close friends. There were many Brahmin life members of the Sanstha. After assassination of Gandhi, the head master, G. T. Joshi was in trouble. He was receiving threats from non-Brahmin communities. The menace terrified Joshi. He wrote a letter to Bhaurao describing the menacing situation he was encountering. As soon as Bhaurao received the letter, he made necessary arrangements to stop the threats against Joshi. He sent a volunteer student to protect Joshi at his residence in Astha. The boy said, "We Rayat Sevaks have no caste and religion. To work for the Sanstha is our caste. Joshi sir, you're a Rayat Sevak. It is our duty to protect you. Karmveer is our caste and Rayat Shikshan Sanstha is our religion. Joshi sir, don't get frightened. I'm here with you. Nobody would even touch you and your home. Believe me and be clam and quiet. We're all with you and nothing will happen." And surprisingly, Joshi did not get any threats thereafter. On the other hand, the people interacted with him friendly.

Karmveer was fundamentally an activist of the *Satyashodhak Samaj*. He longed to implement the ideology of the Satyashodhak movement in reality. He was invariably against exploitation done in the name of religion and caste. He further wanted people to keep away from all addictions. Bhaurao himself never went to any of such whims. He encouraged women to pursue education. Once, a girl student came to take admission in Shivaji College. Her family financial position was not good. She was not in a position to pay the fees. Bhaurao met the girl and came to know that she was his friend's daughter. Her father had helped the Sanstha. He thought that if this girl did not get admission, her education would come to an end. She would not achieve what she was aspiring for. He allowed her to take admission without paying fees. Bhaurao wanted women to go forward by seeking education. He wanted them to become independent economically. He encouraged women staff of the Sanstha to pursue education.

Bhaurao aspired to see a society where caste, creed and religious discriminations did not exist. So he encouraged inter-cast marriages. A teacher of the Sanstha wanted to marry a Brahmin girl. But there was opposition from both the families. Raut was Mali by caste. But both of them did not give up. The marriage ceremony was celebrated at Satara. Bhaurao's health was not good. He was suffering from high blood pressure and his legs were swollen. Still, he attended the ceremony because it was an important event for him in setting down new standards for social and cultural transformation. He spoke on this occasion. He said, "Both the bridegroom and bride are highly educated. They know what they are doing. They are hard working persons. So their parents must bless them for their future. I am a supporter of inter-caste marriages. My cousin brother married a Brahmin girl. We must encourage such marriages on larger scales. So, I congratulate the couple for their venture."

Bhaurao did not approve of extravagant expenditure spent on marriage ceremonies. He believed in simplicity. He saw that his students did not spend extravagantly in their marriage ceremonies. He was against the dowry system which was prevalent in his times. He organized various marriages and he took initiatives in them. He was particular about his principles. He saw that whether ceremonies were conducted in simple ways and no dowries were taken or given. His participation in such programmes had social and educational purposes. He achieved two things at one time. In the first place, he made society wiser by providing education and in the second place, he pointed out evil practices of society.

39

Bhaurao took a flag of education on his shoulder. He did his work faithfully. He showed social commitment while he performed his duties. And he succeeded in pursuing it to its desirable destination. He produced temples of learning at innumerable villages and Wadi-vastis. The task was possible only through his innumerable activists and people. Producing committed activities and hard working people was not a simple task. Such people rendered unprecedented services to him. At times, they even neglected their familial responsibilities. to involve in his herculean tasks. He not only got services from them but he also made them to donate to the Sanstha. This was again more difficult work in which he achieved unbelievable success.

Bhaurao took donations from the rich as well as from the poor. He persuaded the Sansthaniks to donate. He got donations from landless farmers also. He made merchants to pay and forced politicians to contribute to his work. The Sansthaniks like Shinde, Holkar, Gaikwad, Pawar, Bhosale, and Nimbalkar came forward to help him. Merchants and industrialists like Shah, Desai, Borawake and Jain extended a helping hand to him in the development of the Sanstha. Bhaurao never felt hesitated in accepting donations from any strata of life. He used funds and services for the development of his Sanstha. Besides, the greatest contribution of Bhaurao was that he produced a race of people who faithfully scarified their lives for the Sanstha. This was his greatest work.

It was because of his towering personality, hundreds and thousands of activisits attracted towards him. They followed him; they followed his ideas and his work. Some of them walked some distance with him. Such smaller tasks of infinite hands transformed the Sanstha into a huge bountiful Bunyan tree. The Sanstha grew into a huge structure. It set down different ideals in the realm of education. Social reformers, educationists, philosophers and thinkers, statesmen, literary figures, people from aboard, the British officers were wonderstruck to see the network of education unknown in the past. So they admired his works and made some contributions.

The British had always been unfavorable to him and his works. They were suspicious about him and did not approve of what he was doing. The CID frequently forwarded reports to the government. The Governor Lamale came to know about his works through such reports.

In 1938, he visited the Sanstha with his wife. Bhaurao's parents were present on the occasion. His father was a government clerk and he did not know that his son has become a limelight personality. Bhaurao introduced his parents to the governor. His father realized that his son was wandering across Maharashtra with a social purpose. "Arre, Bhau, I thought that you were wandering everywhere waywardly; your work has social significance. I always felt it difficult to get an appointment of a collector. But today, the Governor of Bombay himself is at my son's doors. This is the happiest day in my life. I could see it with my own eyes that you have really become a great man." His father realized that his son had really become a person of some substance. The governor Lamane's visit was of an advantage to Bhaurao.

Sardar Vallabhabhai Patel was on Maharashtra tour in 1941. He paid a visit to the Sanstha. Bhaurao's works produced good impressions on his mind.. He said "Bhaurao's Sanstha is an epitome of true democracy. It is like a small plant today but it will grow into a huge tree. Bhaurao's work is immense." Jayprakash Narayan paid a visit to the Sanstha in 1946. He said that Bhaurao's work was an eye opener to the educationalists and politicians. He had shown a new path, a new approach through his works. He said, had he been not in politics, he would have accompanied him in his works.

The Devapur School located in Maan tehsil of Satara district was a unique example of the Sanstha's experimental venture. Bhaurao did an experiment in this school. He admitted children in this school who had criminal history and background. He tried to unify agriculture and knowledge in this school. The school emerged as a guiding force for ten to twelve villages of the region. Students tilled the land of Rajewadi campus. The school had children from Ramoshi and Dhangar tribal communities. Ramoshi community had been registered by the British as a criminal community. Bhaurao was therefore always curious enough to show this branch to renowned personalities to impress them that education can be a powerful tool of social change.

The Finance Minister of India Dr. Joshi Mathai visited the school in 1953. He was impressed by Bhaurao's modest efforts. The Vice-Chancellor of Gujarat University Bhailal Patel, Guruvarya R. P. Sabnis, L. M. Shriknat (Chairman of Scheduled Caste Committee) visited the school. All of them said that it was an extremely difficult task to impart education to such students in an unfavorable condition. They said, "It is absolutely an impossible thing to impart education here. Terrible and utter poverty, all sorts of odds, no interest in education, no income...and in such dire situations,

Bhaurao found out ways. He overcame odds and succeeded in his mission." The communities of the region had largely neutral attitudes to education. They were struck in poverty and faced all odds. Paucity of adequate facilities and no income sources had made them desperate. In such conditions, Bhaurao came out successfully. This was his great contribution. To work in unfavorable situations had become his habit. Internationally recognized educationists paid visits to the Sanstha. Mr. Cope from America visited the head office of the Sanstha, Satara in Feb.1952. Bhaurao organized a felicitation programme on this occasion. Mr. Cope threw light on Bhaurao 's personality, his works and his peculiarities.

He said that he was perplexed to see the expanse of the Sanstha. He described Rayat Shikshan Sanstha as an institution that was produced out of the need of the people. Only books are not taught and learnt here but a book on self-help is written in this Sanstha. He observed that numerous people in the world talk about world peace, but are covertly preparing for war. But this Sanstha in true sense is preparing for peace. Cope said that Bhaurao's composition of personality was made of faith, self-confidence, prophetic vision and commitment.

Mr. Bulganin and Kruschev, the Russion leaders were also profoundly impressed by Bhaurao's works. They invited him to Russia. Bhaurao was suffering from heart problems. Bulganin told Bhaurao that he would give him a strong heart if he visited Russia. Bhaurao said that his friend Karmveer Hiray had given him one hundred area of land and his boys are going to till the land. He required a tractor to plough the land. So he requested Mr. Bulganin to send two tractors for his boys. But the follow up work was not pursued and so Bhaurao did not receive any tractors from Russia.

The devout Gandhi follower Acharya Bhise achieved all-sided rural transformation and started rural industries on the Gandhian principle. He visited Sanstha and was impressed by Bhaurao's works. This was the admiration voiced by one Gandhi follower for another Gandhi follower.

The Broadcast and Information Minister B. V. Keskar said in 1946 after his visit to the Sanstha that Rayat Shikshan Sanstha must be the only Sanstha which practised the principle of self-help and self-reliance. Maharshee Dhondo Keshav Karve blessed Bhaurao's work whereas Sane Guruji described the Sanstha as a smaller manifestation of mother India. Thakkar Bappa visited the Sanstha twice. He said that the Sanstha is an innovative laboratory of Mahatma Gandhiji's ideology. Dr. Babasaheb Ambedkar said that the Sanstha has been an excellent example of educational experimentation and Bhaurao has set down the standards of self-help in the field of education.

Prof. Maulana Azad, Prof. Humayan Kabir, Dr. K. G. Sayyadin visited the Sanstha and offered ten thousand rupees for *Earn and Learn Scheme*. The Finance Minister of India C. D. Deshmukh and his wife Durgabai paid a visit to Shivaji College in 1948. They inaugurated two classrooms of the college. Mr. Deshmukh described Rayat Shikshan Sanstha as a golden mine of social workers in Maharashtra. He said that Bhaurao worked ceaselessly in the field of education with a social purpose and attempted to eradicate untouchability. He did not advertise of what he was doing. He worked like a missionary without making any propagation of his work. So he made a plea to all to come together and carry out his historical works.

Such towering personalities like Acharya Atre, Bhausaheb Khandekar, S. M. Mate, P. L. Deshpande, Justice Gajendragadkar, Sane Guruji and Achutarao Patwardhan admired Bhaurao 's works. This was his true assessment and so more comments are redundant here.

40

Frequent visits of stalwart personalities from different strata of life to the Sanstha became a regular site. Contribution in eradication of casteial discrimination, innovative experimentations in education, social and educational enlightenment, especially in the bahujan communities sparkled Bhaurao's name across the country. Besides, his ceaseless struggle, his visionary approach uplifting downtrodden, the poor and the bahujan communities, his compassion for the hard working, poor and the needy students, his magnanimous traits, and his boundless love for his boys, activists and his working staff, his commitment to the cause of education, his sacrifice, his selflessness and his huge dreams for which he worked tirelessly all his life... all these and many more made Bhaurao a really towering personality in the country. People proposed to celebrate golden jubilee programme as part of respect and admiration to his work. Prof. Humayun Kabir published an article in English on Bhaurao's contributions in education field. The people looked at the Sanstha and Bhaurao's work with respect and dignified attitudes. He got people's recognition; everybody began to say, "Anna's work is really huge!"

"Yes! It is huge! No doubt about it!

"But his work is a little greater than his guru!"

"Do you say so! How is it?"

"You see, Mahatma Jyotiba Phule started a school and Anna who was influenced by him, and he started innumerable schools."

"That's true!"

"Phule made the water storage from his courtyard free for people belonging to varied castes and creeds; whereas Anna taught his students to eat meals together, at time to eat in one dish."

"That's true indeed!"

"Rajarshi Shahu Maharaj started separate boardings for each caste and creed, but Anna started one boarding for all castes and creeds together."

"That's true!"

"The Maharaj at least had some local religions guru, but Anna had no religions guru."

"The Maharaj administered boarding without charging fees, and Anna co-ordinated knowledge and labour and provided dignity to labour. Anna was never a owner of his Sanstha. The boys came forward to look after the Sanstha."

"Anna started schools, where it was just impossible to start. This was really a perplexing thing. So, the government was afraid of him and at times he also gave warnings to the government."

He was a real Karmveer, a great hero of actions! That is what the people called him and that is the most appropriate description of Bhaurao's personality!"

These were the responses and feedback that triggered from common man's consciousness. His name and fame and recognition reached every corner of the country. The government appointed him on scores of committees. The committees were instrumental for him to enrich his social and educational work. On 26 Jan. 1959, when Padmabhushan Award was conferred on him, he was at Sassoon Hospital in Pune. Bhaurao said that people recognized him as Karmveer; so this government title was an additional feather in his cap. However, he preferred recognition of the masses and his people to the government award.

The news broke out and everyone ran to him. Someone garlanded him; some offered him a bunch of flowers. Some distributed sweets; some distributed fruits and everyone was happy. People gathered could not control their joys. Tears of unbound joys appeared in their eyes. Bhaurao was sick and he was bed-ridden. He had become weak. He was not in a position to get out of bed. Till four in the afternoon, there was an uncontrollable crowd visiting the hospital to congratulate him. He was not able to receive the Padmbhushan Award.

Bhaurao was on the radio to deliver a short speech after he was conferred Padmabhushan. In his short speech, he announced that he must work for the tribal, Dhangar and Ramoshi communities. It is remarkable to note that in spite of his ill-health, his creative powers were still vibrant and his sense of the commitment to the cause of his mission was fresh. The speech was recorded at the residence of Mr. Sanas. This was his first and last speech on the radio.

When Bhaurao was conferred Padmabhushan title, Kakasaheb Gadgil was a little confused. He said who awarded whom. Bhaurao's missionary work enhanced preciousness of the government award. Karmveer Bhaurao Patil all his life served the poor. He gave a pencil and pen in the hands of farming communities who had held a plough. He was responsible for breaking chains of illiteracy. He set down different standards of life in his times. According to him, the meaning of life lies in living for others. One should aspire for huge dreams and work hard for others to transfer them into realities. He took a small bowl without oil and collected oil for it. He showed a path of life to those stumbling in darkness. This was his unprecedented contribution. His work was such that Maharashtra underwent a socio-cultural transformation and the non-Brahmin movement emerged. It was because of his work, the post 1930 era saw a cultural revolution in Maharashtra. On account of his historical contributions, University of Pune recognized his works. He was conferred D.Litt. by the University. D.Litt. is considered as the highest degree in the field of acquisition of knowledge.

The University authorities passed a resolution to award D. Litt to Bhaurao. Wrangler R .P. Paranjape was the Vice-Chancellor of the university. It was at this time, a phone call sent a message that Bhaurao was in Sassoon Hospital suffering from a heart stroke. Dr. Sarojini Babar visited the hospital immediately. Bhaurao was very sick; his face was showing those marks. The university completed all formalities. The Governor's signature was the last rite left out. Fortunately, the Governor Shriprakash was in Pune and he sent a message that he has granted the permission for D. Litt. to be conferred on him.

On 5 April 1959 the Vice-Canceller Wrangler Paranjape, the Registrar and other officials entered the hospital. It was the afternoon time. When Bhaurao saw them, he tried to get up from his bed. The V. C. requested him not to get up but rather lie on the bed itself. Then he informed him the purpose of his visit to confer the degree on him. Saying so, he put on the red gown on him and a garland of flowers. He said, "Anna, you will soon get well and start your future work." Bhaurao was exhausted and his eyes were tired. His face was dried. But his sense of humour was vibrant. He told the V. C. that he never passed in all subjects in an academic year all his school life. Somehow he gradually came up to the sixth class but today, because of this degree, he said he has become a *Doctor*. All those present on the occasion burst out in laughter.

The Governor paid a personal visit to him in the hospital. He sat beside him and took his hand and congratulated him for D. Litt. He talked to him and came to know about his experiment in the education field. Bhaurao's philosophy of education was incorporated through the Earn and Learn Scheme. He wished good health and hoped that he would be all right in a couple of weeks and he took his leave.

Bhaurao's work also flowered in Ahemadnagar district in Maharashtra where he started many branches of the Sanstha. He had produced innumerable activists and workers. Sugar barons, leaders from political parties and common people came forward to respect him. They decided to give one lakh rupees *Thaili*. But his health was not good. He was not in a position to attend the programme. The doctors advised him not to travel. Chintamanrao Deshmukh, the Vice President and the Trustee of the Sanstha was going to preside over the programme. Dr. Dhananjayrao Gadgil attended the programme on behalf of him.

The programme was organized in Ahemadnagar. The President of the Satkar Samiti Sou. Hirabai Bhapkar read out the text in praise of his works attempted during the last five decades. Dr. Gadgil accepted the Thaili and the *Manpatra*. Chintamanrao Deshmukh spoke on the occasion. He said that Karmveer was a great educationist. He was a dynamic activist. He believed in the epigram that work is worship. He said that Karmveer possessed prophetic visionary outlook like a Rushi from the ancient times. He dreamt of a non-violent revolution worked out through the instrument of education. He attempted to establish social equality by education. He succeeded in attaining his aims and objectives. His dream came true. But Karmveer ceaselessly worked for five decades consistently for his dreams. He is a *Karmyogi* of modem Indian. He gave a pragmatic approach to the social revolution. He is therefore one of the great personalities of our country who participated in the nation building and in the making of modern India. The unique feature of his work was that he never depended on the government support. He persuaded masses to participate in his works.

Dr. Gadgil said that Bhaurao succeeded in attaining social integration and equality through his works. He empowered the society and achieved social integration and equality. He showed a new paradigm of education affordable to a poor country like ours and he set down new standards of national education.

On 7 May 1959 Chintamanrao Deshmukh, Dr. Dhananjayrao Gadgil, Sou. Bhapkar and others met Bhaurao in Sassoon Hospital. They talked on scores of topics. Chintamanrao told him that a person of his stature was necessary for progress of our country. His experience and guidance as an educationist would help the nation to build new pillars of national education. He wished to plan out a new pattern of education for the rural population of Indian society but that day never rose up.

Bhaurao's health gradually deteriorated day by day. He had been working consistently since 1909. He worked without rest for more than five decades. He carried pangs of common man on his shoulder. He carried a bundle of anxieties for common man with him. The strength of the huge bunyan tree had its own limitations. How far it could withstand so huge load? How many years? In a period of five decades, Bhaurao travelled extensively and intensively for donations to start new branches of the Sanstha. He searched rural talents and accommodated them in his boarding. When he took such efforts, his pocket was always empty. How did he do this? This was indeed possible for person like only Bhaurao. The budget of the Sanstha was just thirty rupees in the beginning. It exploded into thirty five crores of rupees in 1988. In 2009, it was more than five hundred crores. This did not happen easily. He worked ceaselessly all his life. What he did is beyond one's own imagination. This mind and body consistently was involved in the mission. Naturally, how long this mind and body would tolerate innumerable pangs! Obviously, it had its own limitations.

Besides, Bhaurao did not pay any attention to his health right from the beginning. He worked consistently to give shape to his vision. Health problems appeared to him trivial in the face of his work. He never took them seriously. On the country, he was more sensitive to health problems of his boys. He took care of his boys. He knew exactly problems of his boys, their wounds, injuries and so on.

His hands provided warmth, love, affection and compassion to others. These hands shouldered huge bundles containing eatables for his boys. These hands held a stick too to beat them and show them a righteous path. They held a pencil to teach them. They held a duff to play music and a plough to till the land. His hands were always ready to embrace agonies and sufferings of others. They enlightened society that was in slumber. Such were Bhaurao's hands! But now they were tired.

He had health problems right from 1942. But they took graver forms after 1948. He was treated sometimes at Pune. Doctors forced him to rest. He went for rest at Mahabaleshwar or on some occasions he was at Wai Mission Hospital. However, he never disturbed his busy schedule. He did not follow the diet prescribed by his doctors. Subsequently, it led him to go through two heart attacks. At last, he was in Sassoon Hospital.

Bhaurao was physically a strong man from the beginning. Right from his boyhood days, he took physical exercises. But in course of time he got entangled in his busy schedule. His habit of physical exercises slowly slid away. His eating habits were moderate. But even then he had heart problems. His busy schedules did not permit him to take rest. Whenever he was forced to take rest at Mahabaleshwar, he said that he was an activist and he could never like to rest like a rich person. He called it luxury and it made him restless. Work itself was some kind of rest for him. His students did not agree with him. Nevertheless, he was forced to take rest. Then, he told his students that they should not tax the Sanstha by expenses of his hospitalization.

He travelled extensively all his life to collect funds for the Sanstha but he did not want that you spend it for personal use. For he knew it well that the funds belonged to the society. He was very sensitive about it. He insisted to spend it for the educational purpose of his boys only. He was rather orthodox about it. His friends like Ramchandra Pawar of Tadsar always paid his medical bills.

He did not take rest after the discharge from the hospitals. No sooner did he feel a little better than he began his undone work. The accumulated stress of work sent him again and again to hospital. He faced similar problems in 1955. He was sent to Jahangir Nursing Home in Pune. Dr. Koyaji treated him and he was all right. He was on strict diet in the hospital. His food in the hospital was neither chilly nor tasty. He never liked such food. He called his boys and ate a bhakari, bhaji and chutney etc. On such occasions, he asked his boys to close the doors of his room. Moreover, he did not take medicines on time. M. M. Katkar and Rambhau Kumbhar nursed him when he was at Jahangir. He returned to Satara as soon as he felt a little better.

The Silver Jubilee Programme was celebrated on 3 November 1955 at Kirloskarwadi. He had worked in this factory when he was a boy. He wanted to attend the programme. Arrangements were done. Dr. Malase of Satara examined Bhaurao and he advised him not to go for this programme. But he did not take the doctor's advice seriously. He attended the programme and also delivered a short speech on this occasion. And when he came back to Satara, he again fell sick. He was on the bed for six days in the Sanstha office. At last, after consultations with doctors, it was decided that he must be sent to Sassoon. He was not ready. Dr. Sarojini persuaded him. She told him that she knew Dr. Bodhe and he was familiar to her. Dr. Bodhe was the head of one department in the hospital. He treated him. Then Bhaurao became ready to go to Sassoon.

He was suffering from blood pressure. His heart was swollen. Dr. Modi, the head of the hospital examined him. He was surprised to notice the swelling of his heart. He said that this man was still alive only on his will power.

He went through severe heart problems in January 1956. The blood pressure shot up. He fell unconscious. However, he kept talking half consciously about Sanstha. When he improved a little, he insisted on returning to Satara. The people attending him did not allow him to do so. They knew it that on his return to Satara, he would once again start his stress schedule and avoid medications. So, they thought it better if he continued to stay in the hospital. Katkar, Pandurang Saravade, Rambhau Kumbhar, Principal Swami, Principal Nikam, Attar and Bhaurao's students were at his service. Several others huddled together to meet him. They brought fruits, flowers and sweets. He distributed them in the hospital.

Principal N. D. Patil paid a visit to Bhaurao in the hospital. He was the student of Bhaurao. Both talked on several issues of the Sanstha. Bhaurao told him that at any cost his Sanstha must survive. It is a historical need of the time. When the need of the time might end, the Sanstha would also end. He told that activists like him must support the Sanstha. He also told him that he would not surrender before anyone and never ask anyone to do a favour to him.

On 5 May 1959, Bhaurao called his grandsons. He gave them sweets and talked to them compassionately. On 7 May, he was felicitated in Ahemadnagar. Dr. Gadgil accepted the Manpatra in his absence. On 8 May, Bhaurao wrote letters to Yashwantrao Chavan and Chhatrapati Shahaji Maharaj.

He wrote to Yashwantrao Chavan that he had little

hopes of his survival. The Sanstha was expanding its network. Its work was rapidly rising to new heights. He was worried about the Sanstha's future. He appealed to Mr. Chavan to take interest in the Sanstha, so that he would breathe his last happily. He congratulated him for giving fee concession for low income group students. He also wrote to him that the Sanstha was donated one hundred acres of land near Devapur. He wanted to work out a good plan for it.

It was Saturday on 9 May 1959. It was a day of Shivjayanti celebration. People were paying visits as usual. Bhaurao had his breakfast. He went through the letters of the day. Saravade, Patil, Katkar helped him to move to the bathroom. He walked independently without support. He had to take support of the wheel chair every day. He greeted the patients around him with his hands folded. Perhaps it was his farewell to everyone.

After he came back to his place, Dr. Modi and Dr. Sule examined him. He was given medicine. He had some problem of urination. After that Mr. and Mrs. Magdum met him. They talked on education and its relationship with social progress. Dada Patil of Karjat also met him and he too chatted with him for some time. At 12.00 noon, Sarvade give him milk and a chapatti. Bhaurao ate it happily. He also said social work was one kind of thankless job. But you have to work without getting tired. So he said we must continue this work.

While he was talking to Dada Patil, his body showed severe pains. It agonized and began writhing in pains. The pains went beyond his capacities. He thumped his legs; his face went berserk. Dr. Modi came immediately. He was given oxygen and injection but it did not work. Bhaurao breathed his last. He was talking to Dada Patil a few minutes before and now he was no more. He was now in complete oblivion.

The news spread like a whirlwind in Pune. Gadgil,

Sanas, Shedge, Paranjape, Ghate, Maharshi Karve reached Sassoon immediately. Dr. Modi informed to the Sanstha that he would make arrangements to take the body to Satara safely covering it by ice. The body came to Satara by 7.30 in the evening. There was a mammoth crowd to have the *darshan* of their departed teacher. Yashwantrao Chavan, Babasaheb Kher came to attend the funeral the next day. Bhaurao's mother came from Kolhapur. A huge procession started from Dhanini's Baug. At 12.00 noon, on 10 May, his body immersed into infinite. Thus, a great soul left for a journey of unknown darkness. But he did not forget to give us a fistful of light.

Glossary

Aaee	: A vocative used for mother in Marathi
Anna	: A vocative used for an elderly brother in a Maharashtrian family
Annas	: 1940's and 50's Indian currency; sixteen annas was equal to one rupee
Alankar	: Golden ornaments; here adding to beauty
Amavastya	: Moonless night
Bhaujan Hitay	: Social happiness lies in social welfare.
Bahujan Sukhay	:
Baggi	: A short cart
Bhaji-Bhakari	: Bhakari is the staple diet of a Maharashtrian, made from the Jawar dough and Bhaji is a vegetable with which bhakari is eaten
Bharud	: A folk song
Dakshina	: A Brahmin priest is given some money or useful household articles
Darbar	: A palace
Dholakiwala	: A person who plays a rhythm instrument like *dholak*
Fasting day	: A day in a week is spent fasting in the name of a particular god
Ghongadi	: A type of blanket made from sheep wool

Gurudakshina:	Fees that students give to his teachers in the form of money or gifts
Jeens	: Bedding made from thick textured sheep wool
Jalase	: A programme based on folk music, drama and songs
Lawani	: A folk song
Mandal	: A group of people who think alike and want to go for some charity work for welfare of the society
Mangwada	: A place where the Mang people lived
Manpatra	: A document admiring Bhaurao's works
Mot	: A big water bag made from local leather; an arrangement to fetch water from a well for irrigation of land with the help of oxen.
Muhurta	: A holy or pious day when some significant work is to be commenced
Nanadanvan	: A paradise like place
Nidhis	: Award in terms of large funds as a financial assistance to the Sanstha
Padwa	: New Year Ceremony according to Hindu Calendar
Pahilwans	: wrestlers
Pancha (Pl: panchas)	: A thin piece of a white linen used as a short towel
Patilaki	: To become head of the village and take on several responsibilities of the village and make efforts to resolve them.
Pital/Pithal or: Zunaka	: A typical Maharashtrian dish
Powada	: A folk song
Prasad	: A morsel of eatable given to the devotees in the name of God
Pravachan	: A religious sermon
Punav	: Full moon night

Punyakama	: Good work leading to development and progress of the society
Sansthaniks	: Local kings and the rich
Satyashodhak	: An important social movement initiated by
Samaj	Jyotiba Phule in the nineteenth century Maharashtra
Savarn	: People who do not belong to the backward
Communities	communities like Chambahr, Mahar, Mang etc.
Shringar	: When girls beautify themselves; performing make-up while girls attend festive functions
Slokas	: A type of a precise poem prevalent in the Medieval Indian literature
Thaili	: A fund for promotion of the missionary work
Vag	: A folk drama
Vahini	: A vocative used for wife of an elderly brother in a Maharashtrian family
Wada	: A huge well-built house, a mansion like place
Wadars	: Labourers who belong to the backward sub caste called Wadars and by tradition they break stones.
Wadi-vastis	: Small habitations around a village

About the Source Text Author

 Dr. D. T. Bhosale is a senior retired professor of Marathi language and literature. He worked in Rayat Shikshan Sanstha's varied colleges. He has written around more than forty books in Marathi; they include critical and creative texts like two novels, seven anthologies of short stories, two biographies, five books on folk literature and six books on criticism. His biographical book on Sant Gadage Maharaj entitled, *Lokottar* (2007) published by Granthali got wider acclaim and recognition. He has also edited about more than fifteen books in Marathi on fiction and criticism. His primary interest in writing has been to manifest issues of rural life and questions of farming communities. He won several awards for his writings and held many distinguished roles of honour in Savitribai Phule Pune University, and Shivaji University, Kolhapur during his career. Dr. Bhosale is also a popular columnist; he writes in leading Marathi dailies on important issues of language and culture.

About the Translator

Dr. Deepak Borgave is a senior teacher of English language and literature. He has been teaching to UG and PG since 1979. He holds a Ph. D. in *Translation Studies*, an M. Phil. in *Modern British Poetry* and a *Post Graduate Diploma in the Teaching of English* from EFL, University Hyderabad. He has translated several literary and non-literary works till the date. An English translation of the source text by Adv. Ram Kandge entitled, *Loknete Sharadrao Pawar* has been translated and published by him in November 2015.

He visited University of Reading and University of Kent, UK and Paris, France to present papers on *Translation* and *Culture Studies*. His papers have been published in the UK and US University Journals. His areas of interests are Literary Translation, Contemporary Trends in Criticism, Linguistics, Comparative Literature, Post-colonial Translation Studies and Indian Literature in Translations. At present, he is working as the Associate Professor in the Department of English, Mahatma Phule Mahavidyalaya (Pimpri) Pune.